AMANDA GOLDBLATT

LAURA ADAMCZYK

HARDLY CHILDREN

Laura Adamczyk lives in Chicago. Her fiction has won awards from the Union League Civic & Arts Foundation of Chicago and has appeared in *McSweeney's, Guernica, Hobart, Chicago Reader, Salt Hill, Vol. 1 Brooklyn*, and other publications. *Hardly Children* is her first book.

HARDLY CHILDREN

HARDLY CHILDREN

Stories

LAURA ADAMCZYK

FSG Originals

FARRAR, STRAUS AND GIROUX | NEW YORK

FSG Originals
Farrar, Straus and Giroux
175 Varick Street, New York 10014

These stories previously appeared, in slightly different form, in the
following publications: *Chicago Reader* ("Gun Control"), *Copper Nickel*
("WANTED"), *Guernica* ("Girls"), *McSweeney's* ("The Summer Father"),
Salt Hill ("Needless to Say"), *Sycamore Review* ("Intermission"),
Vol. 1 Brooklyn ("Give and Go"), and *Washington Square Review*
("Here Comes Your Man").

Library of Congress Cataloging-in-Publication Data
Names: Adamczyk, Laura, 1981– author.
Title: Hardly children : stories / Laura Adamczyk.
Description: First edition. | New York : Farrar, Straus and Giroux, 2018.
Identifiers: LCCN 2018006354 | ISBN 9780374167899 (pbk.)
Classification: LCC PS3601.D365 A6 2018 | DDC 813/.6—dc23
LC record available at https://lccn.loc.gov/2018006354

Designed by Richard Oriolo

Our books may be purchased in bulk for promotional, educational, or
business use. Please contact your local bookseller or the Macmillan
Corporate and Premium Sales Department at 1-800-221-7945, extension
5442, or by e-mail at MacmillanSpecialMarkets@macmillan.com.

www.fsgoriginals.com • www.fsgbooks.com
Follow us on Twitter, Facebook, and Instagram at @fsgoriginals

10 9 8 7 6 5 4 3 2 1

FOR VICKI AND ROSE

CONTENTS

HARDLY CHILDREN

WANTED

I F ASKED, I WILL NOT say that I love children. Nor that I particularly do not love children. I'm not one of those who yells at parents to keep a better eye out when their kids run into the street or push into my pelvis at the coffee shop. I will instead say, if asked, that I notice them around— when I'm on my way to work or returning from the store—that I see their presence, I know undeniably that they exist, but that I have no real opinion on them one way or the other. People will assume that, like all women my age, I must have strong feelings in this regard. But, to me, they are only smaller, more naive adults—difficult to predict but easier to talk to.

This morning I saw the posters around the neighborhood. This is a medium-sized town. Not so small that I could tell you the names of my neighbors or they mine, which I never fully considered until now, but small enough that a parent could discover a problem with her son or daughter and then talk to a friend who knows a guy who is a retired sketch artist or who took an art class at the community college, and ask him to draw a picture and help staple copies of that picture to a few dozen telephone poles. This is how things can be handled here, though I've never taken advantage myself. I don't talk much. I work in the back, as they say. And it's true. This afternoon I'm making a mound of chopped onions; later I'm responsible for converting radishes into roses, the most creative thing I'll do all day. Though it's nothing compared to putting pen to paper. The artist of the poster captured a familiar unkempt androgyny in his creation's face. Eyes deep within sockets and high cheekbones, a sharp hollowness beneath. Have I seen this man? the poster asked. The skeletal face bones, the limp shoulder-length hair give it away. I've never looked like a woman, but most adults figure it out eventually. In the meantime, I'm keeping my distance. I'm avoiding mirrors.

The other day at the park I was in the swings that are set away from everything else—the jungle gym, the baseball field. As I pushed myself slowly with a foot on the ground, a boy approached and sat one over, pumping his legs lightly. It was a little boy who looked like a little girl. He wore white tennis shoes with pink swirls and a pair of teal gloves. He'd broken away from his friends who were running across the jungle gym bridge and squeaking up the metal slide, their screams ringing out wild and open like they were joyfully murdering each other. He asked me why I was swinging by myself and I asked him why *he* was swinging by *him*self. He dropped his legs, let his body go slack, then started pumping. I like to! he said. And then he went at it with vigor, as if to prove it to me. He had perfect form: knees together, toes pointed. Sometimes he threw his head back, letting his arms go straight. He was going at a nice pace when I said, Though sometimes it gets lonely, swinging by yourself. At first I didn't think he heard me, but then with jagged breath he said, You should just swing! And so I did, moving my legs, leaning my torso, back and forth, getting up to such a height that in each forward peak, before the slack chain went taut and gravity jerked back at me, I felt weightless, suspended. Then I mimicked his rhythm until we were synced up—legs mirroring legs; arms, arms. When he noticed, he cried out, We're married!, got in a few more good pumps, and jumped off the swing, landing cleanly in the spread of dirty pebbles below. I brought myself to a stop, then clapped.

Beautiful! I said. Ten points!

He smiled with the proud glee of a gymnast in her prime. He walked up to me, his mouth open in a breathless smile. I'm going to go over there now, he said.

What's your name? I asked.

Chad, he replied.

I put out my hand and he shook it once, twice, as though he went around shaking hands and introducing himself to folks all the time.

Nice to meet you, Chad, I said.

Nice to meet *you*, he said.

He was geared up, ready to run, so I asked as quickly but as delicately as I could: Chad, can I have a hug?

A hug?

We're married now.

You're weird! he cried out, laughing.

That's what everybody says. I turned my head down.

Oh, he said. His waning breath told me he was coming down from his excited peak. I kept my eyes on his shoes and let go a deep sigh. He must have come to some realization about adult loneliness and feeling, because those shoes stepped forward, and the boy in them opened his arms and then closed them on me like I were an old stuffed animal. I kept us there for as long as I could; he did not give any resistance. There's no way to know, I think now, what was happening inside my body. I kept my hands at his back, holding as still as possible. There was a sense of one belonging to the other, a good sense. When I felt his arms easing away, I let him.

Head down, voice quiet, he asked, Are you a teacher?

I work in a restaurant, I said, feeling sick. My life was far away just then, but not far enough. That's how I know that I'll have to answer some questions soon. About love. About how the opposite of desire is not hate, only the absence of desire. Before the boy walked away, I said, Keep doing what you're doing, Chad. It's not always good to become something else. He was only an arm's length away, but it was like he'd already turned his back to me.

Now I perform each action as though it might be interrupted. I stretch plastic over tubs of diced vegetables; I defrost shrimp in the refrigerator instead of the sink. I imagine them walking in quietly, only the squeak of leather, the tap of their polished shoes giving them away. If they cuff me, I won't resist. I'll shape my face into a mild, unreadable thing. But if they ask me to take a walk, to come with them and have a chat, I'll do what I have to do— stiffen my body, turn my fingers into fists, anything to make them put their hands all over me.

GIRLS

I T WAS THE SUMMER our parents got divorced. Mary was five, I was eight, and Ronnie was ten. Five, eight, and ten. Even before Mom told us, the house entered a fevered state—the hot air thrumming, the walls damp with fuzzy moisture. She had a way of trying to keep my sisters and me from unpleasantness, and in those long, hot weekends, she would send us from the house. *Girls, go ride your bikes*, she said. *Go play with the neighbors.* The rich neighbor kids with their freckled noses and heads of thick, preppy hair, cut short and boyish—they ignored us, did not once invite us over. We viewed them as one might celebrities, as people who you recognized but who did not, in turn, recognize you. Around their property ran a tall white fence, and from our backyard we could hear them across the street splashing in their pool; we could see their heads popping up above that fence as they leaped from the diving board into the water. For me, the scenes taking place inside that yard were central, real, and whatever was happening inside our home—Mom closing the front door despite the heat, Dad talking fast and sharp into her ear—was the thing keeping us on the other side of their fence.

Our dad was a drinker—a *drinking man*, I would overhear my mom say—and during his last weeks before leaving, he drank more. I remember but one night from this time. Mom was working late at a dentist's office an hour out of town, and Dad was in the living room recliner, tilting his head back to drink from a can of beer, then setting it down on the side table. His drinking seemed to coordinate with the setting of the sun: one gold can and then another disappearing, the light outside moving from blond dusk to dark. I felt uneasy, but couldn't say why. We were doing just what we always did—Ronnie and Mary and I sat drawing quietly at the dining room table, looking up from time to time to the TV in the other room—but our movements felt slow and intentional, as men floating weightlessly in space.

After the local news, Ronnie rose and turned on the tall lamp in the corner. It was like someone folding shut a large book, the pages closing heavy and certain—and upstairs a door creaked open—because with the lamp on I realized what was bothering me: all the shades were up. The night had fully darkened and the lights were burning in the house so that we could not see the world outside, but it could see us. Ronnie squinted at her reflection in the window. She was tall and slender, already moving past the white-blonde hair Mary and I still wore, the soft flesh of our adolescence. Because of Ronnie's height and graceful posture, people often thought her older than ten. She occupied that maturity most naturally in our mother's absence, giving Mary her baths and telling us—as with a guiding hand on the smalls of our backs—when to brush our teeth, when she thought we hadn't eaten enough. I often felt myself waiting for her to tell me what to do.

Putting a hand on her hip, she looked into the living room, where Dad's head had fallen back, his eyes closed and feet up. At the table Mary yawned and scratched the side of her neck.

Ronnie said, Come on, Mary. Let's go to bed. I'll read you your book.

The two of them trudged slowly upstairs, Ronnie's hand on her shoulder. I went into the living room, dark save for the light of the television. Dad's face was small, his cheeks and chin bony, scattered with blond, wiry hair. When I think of him now, I see him as I did that evening, his face still, yet seeming to move away from me, as though at the end of a long hallway.

I put my hands on his arm.

Dad. I pushed gently. Dad, wake up.

He sighed, opened his eyes to dull slits, and said my name: Frannie. Then he crossed his arms over his chest and closed his eyes. I climbed over the side and wedged myself between him and the recliner's arm.

Hey, there, he said, shifting, putting me in an awkward embrace, my arms pinned to my sides, my head hard against his bony shoulder. If he hugged me, it was like this—uncomfortable and stiff—like he didn't know quite how to do it, as though I were a pillow he held on to for some absentminded comfort. His breathing grew sleep-heavy, his arms loosening, and my body began to slide into a crease in the chair, its fake leather cool and slippery. I felt a sharp fear that I was falling into an irretrievable space, that I would fall and fall and forever be away from Mom and Dad and Ronnie and Mary. I imagined a blackness so complete that it erased even their memory of me. They would not notice my absence, I decided. They would not even look. Then Dad cleared his throat and said, Go to bed, Frannie. He turned away, curling deeper into sleep, and I unwedged myself from the chair and went up to my dark bedroom.

. . .

HE LEFT THE FOLLOWING WEEK with little fanfare. I don't remember boxes being filled or boxes carried from the house or the image of his car loaded with boxes. I remember only weeks later, my mother talking on the phone to some unknown listener, her whisper crisp with intent: He had his problems, she said. It was my choice, but truth be told, he couldn't *wait* to leave. He was just itching to get gone. A man unto himself, as they say. It sounded like she'd listened to the country station for too long and had internalized its string of sassy, heartbroken-woman clichés.

She started working Saturdays at the dentist's office in town. Buying school supplies and new clothes hadn't been easy before, but now, even with child support, I felt the weight of her steady denials at the grocery store, the pharmacy. *No. No*, she would say quietly and look away, pushing the cart out ahead of her. Saturday mornings she would drive us out to the edge of our small farming town where my great-grandmother lived in a white clapboard house at the intersection of two gravel roads. One road ran out into corn and dust and hot light, and the other snaked between a shadowy forest and muddy creak, the latter aptly named Widows Road. My great-grandfather died in that house before Ronnie was born, a heart attack felling him as he was returning from work.

The steel-gray mailbox at the front of the property bore his name, BULLOCK, the block letters scrawled angry and childlike.

Through the house's front door were the living room, a dark hallway and pantry, kitchen, and then back door, which opened out onto a treeless swath of sun-bleached grass. We had been told that it was bad luck for the doors of a house to line up in this way, for someone to be able to stand in the threshold of one and see clear through to the other. Something about good spirits too easily entering and then exiting the house. But there was no changing it. Even after a man from down the road snuck in the back one afternoon and went through Grandma's fridge, she kept both doors open for the breeze.

In the afternoons when she watched her soaps in the living room—the volume turned to its highest setting— my sisters and I would creep up to the second floor, the steep wooden stairs hidden behind a crystal-knobbed door off the kitchen. A closed door at the top of the stairs, and on the other side, a series of rooms, a separate apartment that, by then, Grandma rarely entered. When I think of those rooms, I am alone in them. Just as in dreams, I am the sole protagonist. It is Me and the Rooms. Me and Them. I see the low ceiling and the living room's long mauve couch without anyone sitting there. But I know I am wrong. I was too scared of the space to have ever ventured up without Mary or Ronnie, the three of us on hands and knees, crawling, searching. Still, in my memory, when I see a dead cockroach behind the flower stand—crisp, flipped onto its back, legs curled—I am the only one who sees it, it is always my small fingers picking it up.

The whole place was furnished—the couch, a Formica table in the kitchen, a small black television on a short stand—but it was otherwise blank. Mom had told us that the space was once rented out to itinerants. *Drifters*, she said, men looking for work on the surrounding farms or passing from one side of the country to the other. But after my great-grandpa died, Great-Grandma decided she didn't want people coming and going, and she closed it up.

We would bring our books or poke around to see what we could find: a stack of yellowed *Farmer's Almanacs* and *LOOK* magazines next to the couch, empty mousetraps inside the kitchen cabinets. Other times we'd sit at the kitchen table and play house. Ronnie was the father and I was the mother and Mary was the child. Ronnie would boss me and Mary would pretend to cry or get worked up and cry for real and I would say, Shush shush shush, little child. And Ronnie would say things like, Baby, you'd better hush, or, Wife, it's time for you to make me supper. Because I'm the man of the house, that's why, despite never hearing anything like it from our parents' mouths. Ronnie would pretend to read the paper and I would pretend to wash the dishes and Mary would draw the three of us standing before a blank landscape, a single, uncurving line, and when we heard the theme music change on Grandma's TV, we would snake back downstairs with our tracing paper and crayons and books, and refill the spaces on the living room floor or couch where our bodies had once been, as though we'd never left.

IT WAS A HOT SATURDAY. Ronnie and me on the living room floor, pushing around a set of cars Great-Grandma had saved from old Cracker Jack boxes. Mary asleep on the couch with her head in Great-Grandma's lap. She was too old for regular naps, but Grandma still laid her down after lunch and stroked her hair until she fell asleep. Mary's thumb was in her mouth—a habit no one was trying very hard to break in her—and her white-blonde bangs had fallen over her eyes. I wanted to reach out and smooth the hair away from her face, but before I could, the roaring theme music of *Days of Our Lives* opened its mouth and swallowed the living room: *Like sands through the hourglass, so are the days of our lives . . .* Mary woke, shifted, and whined. She may have gone back to sleep. She may have joined us on the floor, running parallel lines with our car wheels through the thick green carpeting. She may have followed us when

Ronnie and I rolled down the hallway, opened the door to the stairs, and closed it behind us, ascending.

Just inside the entrance was the door to the bedroom. It was the door we would not open—by its position in the apartment, the room would be windowless, dark and airless—so when we saw upon entering that the door was cracked, Ronnie said, Oh. And I echoed her *Oh*. And Mary, who might have still been downstairs with Grandma's fingers in her hair, said nothing. I felt the same mix of fear and excitement as when we played hide-and-seek with our cousins and I would sit squatting in the back of a closet or behind a chair, crawling into some space not meant for human bodies. That tingling feeling of simultaneously wanting to giggle and needing to pee. Like before a thunderstorm when you say, *It's going to rain*, and two beats later it does, and you don't know whether it was your own premonition or just a couple of early drops falling on your arms, because we passed the open bedroom door—that tingling still alive up and down my back—and rolled into the living room, where we saw the man sitting on the couch.

Ronnie stopped her car and sat up on her haunches, and I, just behind her, stopped and sat up. Mary, who might not have followed us up, who might have followed us up and then left once entering the room and seeing the man, whispered, Who's that?

The man wore a three-piece suit and a white collared

shirt. We were close enough to see that his shoes were not new, but still clean, well-kept, buffed to a Sunday shine. People did not dress this way in Wilmington. It was mostly farmers in blue jeans or women in stretch pants with the cuffs stuffed into their shoes. The only people who wore suits were the town's two lawyers on Water Street and Mr. Reeves, who owned the funeral home behind the diner. Even so, the man did not look like any other man we knew. He did not have the large, bony nose of my father or his sandy blond hair or short stature. He did not have my father's casual, sloppy way of sitting, and he did not have my father's extra beer flesh around his middle or his sleepy blue eyes.

Instead, the man was tall and slender, with a head of thick, wiry hair that might have been brown or black, his eyes no color I could name.

Um, excuse me, Ronnie said. She used her adult voice with her nose up, hands folded in her lap.

Moving only his head, the man looked down to regard us, his face the gray of a stone worn smooth by water.

Girls, he said. As though he were about to address us. *Girls* . . . Or with merely a sense of recognition, as though we were a pack of gazelles and he a man viewing us through a lens, pointing a long, thin finger out: *I see . . . girls. Just there.* And he said, *Girls*, not *Girl*, which is how I know that I was not alone that day, probably never alone in that room, despite my wont to blot out Mary and Ronnie and even the man himself from any of these memories.

What have you girls got there? the man asked, nodding down to the floor.

I looked to see what was in my hand.

Cars, Mary or I said, while Ronnie shot me or her or us a reproachful look.

Excuse me, who are you? Ronnie asked. She had her sassy mouth on, but was still trying to be kind, as though the man were one of the rich neighbor kids who wouldn't play with us.

I'm the man of the house. He opened his arms, like Moses parting the Red Sea.

Ronnie raised an eyebrow.

I'm a friend of Mrs. Bullock's, he said.

Mrs. Bullock was our great-grandmother. And she did not have any friends. Even then we knew she didn't have friends. We knew that sometimes the children from down the road brought her tomatoes from their garden and that sometimes on the mail lady's day off, she would stop by with her kids and visit and make tea for all of them, while my grandmother would tell her about the three of us and my cousins and Bo and Hope and Marlena on *Days of Our Lives*, all in the same breath like those characters were real and were hers and were part of her life.

Now, girls, you should be playing with dolls, not these *cars*. Where'd you get those?

Great-Grandma, I said.

Great-*Grand*ma?

Mrs. Bullock, I said.

He nodded slowly, looking from Ronnie to me then beyond us to Mary or the carpet where she might have once been. Looking back to me, he said, Might I see one of those cars? He leaned down, opening his hand.

In one memory, I never get any closer than this, than placing the tiny blue shell of a tin car in his palm. The man was nowhere close to my great-grandma's age, yet his skin had the same watery translucence, skin that I knew would be soft and loose upon touching it. I placed the car in his palm. I placed the car tire-side down, as if it might drive up his wrist then forearm then shoulder and into his ear. His fingers closed around it.

Woo-ee, the man whistled, holding it up. That's a real beaut'. I don't think I've ever seen such a fine automobile. Such a fine, *tasty*-looking car.

Tasty? Ronnie said.

The man put the car in his mouth. He clamped his lips down and made his mouth big with chewing. He chewed and chewed and then swallowed, making it disappear.

Ahh, the man said. Thank you, my dear. He smiled at me, showing his teeth then clicking his jaw.

I couldn't help but laugh.

Ronnie shook her head at me. He didn't really eat it, she said.

I certainly did, he said, showing us his palms. A man's gotta eat. Especially in these hard times. So, so hungry. He rubbed his stomach.

I thought about the tin of saltines in the pantry downstairs. I thought about the way Grandma overfed us, but how we ate and ate. The desperate zeal from never having enough. Chicken fingers, macaroni and cheese, bananas, ice-cream bars, sliced peaches with sugar sprinkled on top. One thing after another. Then mints and gum and tea after it was all over, as though we were adult guests and not children, not little bodies with little mouths and stomachs to fill.

Grandma has some snacks, I said.

No. No, Ronnie said, turning to me. Mom had recently become miserly, overly careful with food, and Ronnie had followed suit, tinfoiling anything beyond a spoonful that she hadn't finished.

We don't even know if he's Grandma's friend.

He's hungry, and Grandma barely eats anything.

Just because you don't *see* her eat doesn't mean she doesn't.

I sighed.

Girls, he said again, girls. This time a reproach, this time a preface, an open, hanging sigh. Girls, the man said, I've got an itch.

Instinctively, I scratched the back of my neck.

I'm just *itching*.

So, scratch yourself, Ronnie said.

It's no good, he shrugged. I itch all over. I scratch one place, and it starts an itch somewhere else. It never ends.

That sucks, Ronnie said.

Ronnie, I hissed, poking her side. We weren't supposed to say *suck*.

Ronnie? he asked, raising an eyebrow.

Veronica, she corrected.

Veronica, he said, and, looking in my direction, asked, And who might we be?

Frannie, I said.

Frances, Ronnie corrected.

And Mary, I said to Mary beside me, who might have no longer been beside me.

Ronnie and Frannie and Mary, he said rhythmically. It's like a little song. I'm sorry, he said, putting a hand to his chest, *Veronica* and *Frances* and Mary.

Ronnie smirked.

Now, girls, he said. About that itch. He stretched out his right leg. It's my ankle.

You can scratch it, Ronnie told him.

Can't reach, he replied, and he made a show of stretching down and not being able to get there.

You can so, she said. Just bend your leg.

Can't. Too stiff, these old bones. He wrinkled up his face, leaning back.

I scooted forward.

Frannie.

I gave her a look, then turned back and scratched at the slice of pale skin between his sock and pant leg.

Oh, oh, he said, closing his eyes. You're an expert scratcher, Frannie. You've got it. But then he dropped his leg and put up the other. He opened his eyes: Now it's my other ankle. He shook his foot at Ronnie.

She rolled her eyes and moved forward, scratching at him as one might a stray dog.

Oh oh oh! he said again. Just like your little sis.

And Ronnie gave up a giggle too.

We made a game of it. I itch here! he'd cry and point to his elbow and we'd scratch it. And I itch there! he'd cry and point to his shin and we'd scratch it. I itch here and here and here. We got so worked up, scratching and giggling and tickling, that the whole thing took on a life of its own and started to get away from us, started to bubble over with too much good feeling. But we must not have gotten to a particular itch to his liking, because he dropped his face into a well and said, Scratching around a thing is not the same as scratching a thing. I filled my cheeks and swallowed and felt the bottom of my stomach hollow out. I stood up from the couch, because he looked like a different man just then, a new, older man, and I saw Ronnie stiffen and heard her say, *Frances*, with her same tone of warning, like, *Frannie, stay away from that stove, Frannie, keep your hands inside the car, Frannie, Frances*, but nothing about Mary, who was not even there, who was not there and had never been there the whole time, Mary, who was climbing up onto the couch beside the old, deep man.

WHEN I DRINK, I drink too much. My nights get smudged, as water stains bleeding into newsprint. I can hold on to the headline, the lede, but the details—the walk home, all the in-betweens—lose shape somewhere in the middle of the night, and when I wake in the morning my head is a sponge, the rest of my body a mysterious bruise. It tells me something, and that's usually: there's more that you don't know. Somewhere those nights have burned to ash and I no longer own them, if I ever did. It leaves me with a fear so familiar as to need no introduction, just as one can navigate even the most complicated rooms of her home in the dark.

Mary has been going to therapists on and off since high school. Ronnie says that she doesn't believe in all that, doesn't know what she'd talk about for an hour with a complete stranger every week. *Divorce*, I can hear Mary say, then a man older than her writing it down on a pad of yellow paper. Ah, yes, *divorce*, a puzzle piece, because I've seen those looks of recognition too. I'll be fine and then the furniture in my house shifts. Nothing is where it was before. The bedside lamp and the spider plant start to hide from me. I'll get dark and darker and then go to talk to one of those older men sitting in a beige armchair, and it's like I am very precisely describing a dark gray pool of water. *Divorce* and the man nods and asks me about my week, but we never get to the long shadow I'm pulling behind it.

I call Mary, then Ronnie.

I say, Remember that man at Great-Grandma Bullock's?

And Mary says, What man?

And Ronnie says, There was never a man up there. That upstairs was creepy, though, she agrees. All those dead bugs. I hear her shiver over the phone. But never a man, she says.

I remember the kitchen, Mary says. You guys would yell at me until I started crying. She is matter-of-fact, not angry, but not happy either. In her story, we are the doers of many wrongs, and they're the only things she can remember.

When I think of my great-grandmother's house, I see the things farthest away from me first: the bright rectangle of sunlight coming through the back screen door, her tin of saltines in the hallway pantry, the blue and green living room with the shades pulled down. I see the front screened-in porch, my sisters and me on the tile floor, Grandma on the porch swing, all of us bathed in creamy yellow light. I see the stairs on the other side of the hallway door going up. I see the stairs going up to the second floor and Mary on the couch. Mary on the couch and the man with his hand in her hair and her thumb in her mouth. I see Ronnie's bare slender arms moving out ahead of her, she saying, Mary. Frannie, go. Go downstairs. I see a dark circle in the light brown carpeting and me in the living room downstairs and Mary on the couch with her head in Grandma's lap crying, with Grandma looking sad and saying, It's a hard time for you girls. And I've wet myself. I remember I'm eight years old and on the floor and I've pissed my pants fully, all the way through, no hiding it, but Grandma hasn't noticed yet and I'm not saying anything because I'm too old to piss my pants and it is this knowledge—*too old*— that gets me crying along with Mary, not thinking about my dad sleeping in a different house or my mom and my sisters and me in that big house all by ourselves eating cream of mushroom soup and toast for dinner, and I look to see if Ronnie is crying with us, to see if she's seen that I've pissed myself, to see if I should be feeling what I'm feeling, but she's not there and her cars aren't on the floor and I don't know where she might have gone to. And then the music is changing again on the TV that is turned up too loud and Grandma is saying, Well, shoot, I've seen this one before.

After that summer it wouldn't be a year before Dad would leave the state and stop sending the child support checks, and Mom would move us into an apartment complex behind the grocery store, where I would pine for my old bedroom, while Mary would come to say that she couldn't remember the old house, couldn't remember our father in it. Ronnie took to reading books with dark images on the covers—teenage girls in oversized sweaters staring out windows, a look of overblown anxiety on their faces. I'd pick them up when she finished but would stop reading before anything bad could happen.

Mom did her best to keep things good. We'd go to the movies on discount nights, she sneaking in greasy brown bags of popcorn and cans of soda. But once, during a showing of *Labyrinth*, the manager found her in the dark and asked that the four of us leave. That night at home we'd hear her crying in the bathroom, door shut, Ronnie and Mary and me on the other side. For dinner we ate beans and rice or noodles that looked like hay. Breakfast was oatmeal made with powdered milk, the four of us growing lean and hard, then thin and thinner, our bodies receding to bone, breath quieting to whispers, as though God were trying to erase us.

TOO MUCH
A CHILD

THE OLD MAN WOULDN'T STOP talking about the children. The same old man at the bus stop every morning and usually something about the weather and the kinds of jackets people wore because of it (his was large and khaki, many pockets), but now this heavy, heavy talk.

It reminds me of when I was a child, he said, almost wistfully.

Oh? said the woman beside me. She was short and sour-looking, her hair wavy-dry and going gray, but when the man spoke, her face softened. Bespectacled and bearded, the man talked to everyone there waiting, and instead of each of us standing inside her separate loneliness, he pulled us together as a community.

Kids was always disappearing then, he said. You could lock your door, but it didn't matter. They'd drag them out. There wasn't much you could do. They'd just *take* them if they wanted them.

The woman was listening in close, stitching her brows together—a charged, attentive pity shaping her face. I took out my book. It was large and heavy with gold script on the cover. The story was based on a B horror movie in which a small town is terrorized by a scaled, human-shaped beast I was pretty sure didn't actually exist.

Of course, they took men and women too, not just children, the man said. Old ones and young ones—they did not discriminate! At this he laughed, his eyes going small beneath his glasses.

We had, of course, read about that era when we were in school. The kidnappings and all that went along with them always seemed to have happened elsewhere and deep in the past—it wasn't a history we included our-selves in—but now the old man was pulling this history out, unfolding it, showing us it was not so long ago. History had caught up to us. It had, in fact, become a present-tense kind of situation, and it was this: There was a group of men killing children at night. Going into homes and taking them from their beds. Taking them off the streets. We the people thought we knew who the men were during the day, but because of some technicality we could not arrest them then. They had to be caught in the act. But at night it was dark and they wore hats casting shadows over their faces, and some people thought that the children deserved it. They were not considered the brightest kids in school and were known to steal candy and cigarettes from the corner store, which had always been a rite of passage for people in the area, and even I had once palmed a long, flat apple candy before unwrapping it down the street and letting it form to the roof of my mouth. Stealing from this store was talked about in a weren't-we-crazy-kids-back-then sort of way, but when these kids did it, these *kids-these-days* kids, people likened it to a greater problem with children in general, and they said these children huffed paint too and that some of them had once found a few stray cats and had used them for some dark purpose that had to do with the music they listened to, music whose lyrics we could not understand.

Can't believe this is happening again, the man said. He shook his head. His voice had a certain cadence, a quality that made us like whatever he was saying, even if it was tragic.

What to do, these children? he said. What *can* one do? No one is safe.

You're absolutely right, the woman said. It is so shameful. I'm ashamed to live in this world. She shook her head the way the old man had done.

I had a way of angling from tragedy. I listened but let my face go flat. I wanted people to make a joke of it then put it away, to make it feel less like a scar they were showing me. The most recent kidnapping had been over a week ago, and I hoped it would be the last. But even as I thought it, I knew it wasn't true, knew it wouldn't be the last time, and the real bother wasn't that it wasn't going to be the last time but that the situation wasn't going to change by some old man at the bus stop, as jolly and beloved as he was, talking and sighing and shaking his head, so why not let's not talk about it anymore?

Little Miss, he said, seeming to only then notice me. How old are you?

I'm an adult, I said, and looked down the street. There was a great cube of a clock jutting from the building on the corner—multi-faced so that you could read it from any direction. It always kept perfect time.

It began to rain as my bus pulled up. It took me from the central square and passed through several neighborhoods, each more depressed than the next: gray twoflats with bricks busted out like bad teeth, storefronts behind black bars, trash—heavy and wet—clotting the sewer grates with its pulpy mash, and, on one bent sidewalk, a diapered baby sitting flat on its bottom. The change from straight and square downtown to gray ruin happened so plainly as to serve as a time-lapse example of such collapse, a linear progression charted on an x/y axis: bad, worse, worst.

The bus rattled fast ahead through the rain, the windows shaking as the wheels dipped into each pothole. From behind me came the sound of a marble or ball bearing dropping from some height then rolling along the floor.

Falling apart? the woman in front of me turned to ask. Her lips shaped a wry smile.

Yes, Dear Stranger, I answered in my head. *The world is about to run off the rails. We're all going to get knocked out of orbit, a pool ball chipped off the table. It's not just a feeling I have, Dear Stranger, rather an assurance, a surety, everything so goddamn out of whack that it's no longer a matter of if but when.*

THE BUS TOOK ME to a neighborhood that looked excerpted from elsewhere—an ivied campus where it was eternally autumn, the air sharp and clean, leaves frozen in their most vibrant shade of decay. That this neighborhood was surrounded by the other, grayer neighborhoods served to some as an indicator of all the good that could happen in the world. *A rose blooming in the desert!* For others, it was tasteless bragging, an opulent oasis to which access was highly regulated. I tried not to take sides.

In the rosy neighborhood, I made smart children smarter. They lived in large houses with tall gates, so their parents didn't worry or they didn't worry too much or they worried just the right amount to keep them safe.

As I searched my bag for my room key, a security guard halted his squeak up the hall and said, You're here awful early, young lady. Do you have a pass?

I work here, I said, and handed him my ID.

I see, he said. He took his time studying my two faces. The guard's sleeves stopped at his biceps, his arms bigger affairs than seemed necessary.

Won't happen again, he said.

Doubtful, I thought but didn't say.

In first period, the kids took turns telling me about their summers. Piano lessons. French lessons. A month on an island I'd never heard of. One boy finished a long-beloved book series then buried each volume in his backyard.

My sister told me there are almost endless good books, he said. But none like these.

His face was bony and slight, creating dark pockets of sensitivity beneath his eyes. His hair was chin-length, dark brown, and straight, and he shyly tucked it behind his ear as he talked. I hated choosing favorites, which meant I always did and immediately. His quiet maturity was so stark that it conjured in me the thought of a future when the difference in our ages would shrink to nothing. He, like all of them—as precocious as any darling prodigy— was half my age, me divided in two. I didn't know anything about his parents, save they'd given him the most beautiful name one can to a boy in this language.

During the passing period, I watched the children move up and down the hallway. The girls had long, straight hair, the bright natural blondes and browns of undyed, unaltered youth; the boys were covered in sour, shiny pimples or were girlish and small still—elfin angles in their chins and a flipping bit of hair covering one eye. Our school was an island of beauty and learning and sharing, I told myself, far apart from the mainland of smog and grime and crime, these children princes and princesses of their own sparkling futures.

SOMETIMES I TOOK the train home, a different crowd all the way. None of the old ladies with cagey carts from the bus, clothes humped on backs, or mothers and bundled babies, but people with jobs, moving to and from them. Women in gray pencil skirts and blade-thin heels, hair in sleek curtains down their backs.

There were men too. Men in summer cotton pants and checkered shirts buttoned up, the lips of their belts tucked neatly away. Their faces were shaved smooth or gone to seed, their hair combed slick or left curly-soft. I thought about running my fingers through all that hair. I thought about untucking, unbuttoning, unzipping them. Putting them inside my mouth one after the other. I wondered if, after a brief explanation of my desires, they would permit me this. A nod, a silent assent. And if they denied me, if they recoiled, I wondered if they would comply, acquiesce, *give in* after I explained my feeling, nay, my knowing with an unwavering certainty that this train ride was going to end, and soon, in disaster, hurtling ahead seemingly without conductor, galloping at such a pace that it loosened my gut from the rest of my body. The plane—I wanted to grab them by the wrists—was going down, so they might as well toss their dicks into my face and let me do as I would. We were all in this together.

The air was humid and close from the rain, my skin slick with it. In my book, the protagonist's sister had just gotten her face eaten off by the scaled beast—a low blow, as the protagonist had really seemed to like her sister. Before the train ran express to the nether regions of the city, one last man ducked into our car. He was a tree-sturdy man in a denim shirt and brown boots. Someone in the habit of walking slowly. It used to be that I'd stare and stare at strangers then look away. But when the man at the door finally saw me, I kept at him. I shaped my mouth into something like a smile. He returned the look for only a moment then lowered his head to his newspaper.

At the first stop out of downtown the doors opened and released a sigh of people. The next stop, the same, only less so, the crowd loosening. I got up and stood next to the man by the door. He was somewhere in the soggy middle of the paper, where tucked down in the corner was a black-and-white headshot of a woman in a blazer. The text above her head read, *What of the Children?*

Scary stuff, I said.

What's that?

The weather, I replied. Wind gusts up to seventy-five miles per hour.

I put my hand to my chest and tickled my shirt, a gesture I thought hinted at sensitive concern, one I'd been practicing for some time and that did not go unnoticed by my new, tall friend. His eyes traced a line from my chest to my face. Tilting his head, he said, That's windy, and I knew I wouldn't have to ask him to walk me home.

IN THE MORNING PAPERS: five more children taken. Five more children who had been out the day before— loitering, skateboarding, double-dutching. One child, who was hardly a child anymore, had been out for a walk with his friend, taking in the last day of summer warmth, and a man had not liked the way this hardly child had been walking. The man had used the word "strutting"—*Strutting around in his tennis shoes and T-shirt*—and he told the child, hardly a child, *Son, we need to have a talk*. A hand on his shoulder then several men and several hands on his shoulders and into a white van that had either snuck up just then or been there all along. *In the middle of the day*, the paper said, because this was the important part of the story, the part that was new.

The papers said what had long been speculated but never voiced: All of the men were policemen. Or firemen or congressmen. Somethingmen. A spokesperson for the men said that they knew with certainty who the bad kids were and who the good kids were and which kids would later become bad and which kids were on the fence and therefore should be taken care of just in case. It was instinctual, this knowing, nothing that could be explained in language. If we wanted to stay safe, we had to take their word for it. It held a certain logic, their collective nonexplaining. Nothing revealed and therefore nothing to criticize. Zero equals zero. *Trust us* equals *We can't tell you*. Who were we to question it? We had, after all, given them their uniforms, their nightsticks and badges. We had given them our vote. If they were wrong, what would that say about us?

In an opinion article, a woman said it was all a damn shame. It was certainly hard not to feel bad for the young ones, but adults had a right to be frightened too. Late-night movies and TV series of great childhood uprisings abounded, she said. Early teenagers in dirty jeans and T-shirts with the sleeves cut off, chains and tire irons and fiery bottles in their hands, marching to some midnight destination while a punk rock song built to angry climax. The woman didn't mention how great those films were. How they could light a good fire in you, get you moving to some previously unknown fingers-into-fists feeling. It wasn't just about rebellion, but where the rebellion lived—those movies more about the clothes and the music than anything else. The things that scared the adults and drew the children in.

When I got to the bus stop, they were already talking.

Will not and cannot let this go on, the sweet-and-sour woman said. She looked shorter but more potent, a concentrated version of herself.

The people must rise up, the old man said, leaning back, his hands clasped at his middle. Up up up!

What's the weather doing today? I asked.

The weather, my dear, is changing.

A cold front? I asked. I couldn't take people talking

in metaphors, the weak language of everything-means-something-else.

There's going to be a march, sweet-and-sour said. A demand for information and justice.

I checked the clock on the corner.

You should be interested in this, the old man said.

And why is that?

He eyed me but good. I sensed he was no longer trying to figure me out, rather considering how best to handle me. I liked it better when he complimented my outfits, my seasonally appropriate accoutrements; I always chose just the right ones.

None of us were that long ago children, he said.

Sure, I said, sure. But at least now we have bank accounts. New skirt, I added, and slid open my trench.

He squinted at me, barely noting the skirt or where it stopped above my knees. He looked away.

We are, truth be told, all in danger. Injustice for one is injustice for all.

The woman closed her eyes and nodded.

Tomorrow evening, a man said. Will you be there?

I feel embarrassed yelling things aloud.

Sweet-and-sour snapped her head up, face puckered. Not disappointed so much as shocked that I didn't share her feelings. I opened my book and moved inside it. The town crazy was raving that the beast was a physical manifestation of the evil inside each and every one of them. *Pure evil*, he said, which I was fairly certain couldn't exist outside a sterile laboratory. The old man and woman talked in a new, hushed tone. How strange when strangers tried to step inside you, I thought. Like when men in rags announced themselves to a train car, telling everyone about their lives, their current states of disrepair and what they wanted, needed, God bless, from everyone, which somehow included you, and you kept your head down, reading the same sentence again and again, never quite taking hold of it, and the harder you tried, the more the men's voices got in your ear, the more like they were speaking only to you. Once a man pulled up the leg of his trousers and showed me the wound of him. A red mouth full of cottage cheese, the red mouth saying, *Please, please help me*, and I looked away until he went away.

I sensed the bus-stoppers tightening into a circle. I didn't want to lose them completely, so as I stepped onto my bus, I turned and said, I hope you all have a wondrous day!

MY FIRST-HOUR WAS BLAZING with the news. Trying to get the lesson going, I recapped act two of the play we were reading. A number of noble men and women had recently lost their heads, and everywhere there were bloodstains that just wouldn't come out, but the kids kept circling back.

Are you going to the demonstration? one boy asked the girl next to him.

My parents won't let me, she said.

Mine won't either, but I'm just going to do it.

I have no reason to be downtown.

The library is right there.

Are you going to go? the girl asked me.

Well—I tended to flush when things turned overly personal—these things have a way of becoming very . . . crowded.

But it's a demonstration, one of them said.

Dangerous, then. I stopped, but it didn't seem satisfying, so I did what I always did when I didn't quite know what to say: I turned the question back to them. Do you think it's a good idea to risk it?

A few sidelong glances and the pursing of lips. It was uncanny how little they considered even the simplest questions if they ran opposed to their own convictions. I thought that might have done it, but then my beautiful book burier started talking.

This can't go on, he said. He was looking down. When I think of their families—he stopped, his mind following the thought somewhere the rest of us couldn't go. He shook his head. The gesture echoed the old man and sweet-and-sour, but he had none of their adult importance, the kind that comes from listening too closely to one's own voice.

We have to do *something*, he said, his eyes turned up, large and naive. My face had looked even younger at his age. Adults were forever pitching their voices high to me, but I denied them my childish inclinations, went about my kid business in secret—writing rhymed songs, posing dolls, letting the world silently terrify me. I kept myself hidden, not wanting to conform to any mass noun that might include me.

Nobody ever has to do anything, I said

Not even now? he asked. Not even now?

He was too confused and pleading, too guileless, that look. Too much a child. The rest of them looked the same, their faces cracked open, baby chicks pecking out into the world and me the hen that had warmed them. I never asked for this, I thought, but, Question, question, question mark, their little faces went.

Well, I mean, it's nothing for *you* guys to worry about!

Why not? they asked. Yeah, why not?

You're such good kids, I thought. This type of thing didn't happen to *such good kids*. But I knew it wasn't any kind of thing to say. I also knew that I shouldn't describe the way my head was about to roll off the back of my neck, how certain I was of the end of the world happening so very soon that it was like it had already happened. I put my hand on my stomach and winced.

Act three! I groaned, and flew from the room.

THE WOMAN ON THE BUS was telling the bus how she had a titanium hip and a titanium knee and a glass eye and an implant inside her ear. She had a pin in her thumb, a stent in her chest, and a wig she'd purchased in this very neighborhood. She had no particular audience, getting all the encouragement she needed from the bus's silence. I wondered what was the most of a person that could be made of something else. Hooks for hands and wheels for legs, an iron lung, a metal heart. What's the least amount of human a human could be?

A group of field-tripping daycare children got on at the next stop. Toddling kids no bigger than big dolls, climbing up and in, all holding on to the same red rope.

Sit down, their carewoman called. The bus is about to move!

They scrambled into their seats, legs dangling. The little girl beside me, hair sprouting from her head in a single, round pouf, turned to look out the window, then to me.

Did you tie your shoes all by yourself? she asked.

I nodded.

Oh!

She's a big girl, her watcher said.

I nodded and smiled, and the girl turned to look out the window again. Her ears were impossibly small, as pliable as gummy candy. Somewhere an adult had gotten pregnant and had said, *Okay, yes. Yes, okay, fine.* She had planned it or not planned it and had decided to make a little thing that looked like her. The adult had wanted reassurance that she wasn't so far away from being a child herself. Wanted to make a thing to tell her, *We're not so different, you and me.* But what the pregnant adult did not think about was the way the little thing's face was going to change —from the small, soft version to something hard like burnt cake. The pregnant adult shrank her imagined timeline to include only what I saw now. Who could blame her? I thought about taking the child for myself, taking her by the hand and pointing out the world to her, telling her the names of everything and what I thought any of it meant. I saw myself holding her up in the mirror, she looking into my eyes and saying, *Let's you be me. Let's me be us.* The desire of it was so plain, rising up, bursting out so fast, it was like something I'd spilled all over myself.

I reached over and pinched the toe of her white sneaker, wiggled it, and opened my book in my lap. I liked its weight there. The townspeople had discovered that by channeling their positive energy, they could make the beast change shape, melt, or diminish in power.

They just had to have faith. Of all that had come thus far, this seemed the most unbelievable.

THE NEXT MORNING, the radio told me everything I'd missed. Protesters had gone out into the streets the night before, carrying signs with pictures of the taken. They said, *Show us the men who have done this. Bring them to us.* But there they were. Policemen hidden in plain sight inside their plastic helmets and shields, telling the men and women assembled that they'd assembled incorrectly, had not filed the correct permits five to ten business days in advance and therefore needed to disperse. The people said that justice could not wait. The people said, *Who's next?* A few of them had picked up rocks and put them into the air—dull, impotent thuds against all those plastic shields—and this was reason enough for the men to slide out their thick batons and new crowd-control swords, clearing a path as with a machete through the jungle. They could not quantify it specifically, but there had been significant bloodshed. *Bloodshed*, the radioman said, making it sound like something no longer needed. *Bloodshed*, like snakes ridding themselves of their skin. A spokesperson for the hardly children told the reporter that this was not it, not even close to not it, was even more not it than it hadn't been it before, now with so many new names to add to the signs, and tonight they would meet with the men hidden within uniforms yet again until they got just what they were coming for.

And there were children newly missing, those unaccounted for in the significant bloodshed. Young people from all over the city had come to join the protest and show their support for the taken, only to be taken themselves. They were said to have been snatched from the quieter, more sensitive edges of the protest. I thought of how my fellow teachers called the students their "kids," as though they were all our sons and daughters, and how I didn't think of any other children in that way. Only *my* kids were my kids.

My walk took me past the wooded park, the sun pushing up while mist descended within the trees. A few blocks from downtown I found a shoe on the sidewalk. Just smaller than my hand. White with a silver starburst pulling behind it a glittery rainbow and at the end of its tail a speck of blood. Farther along, a pair of overalls smeared with blood. I thought of the girl on the bus— her edible ears—and it would seem the kind of coincidence that only the most sentimental would create. All along the edge of the park, a breadcrumb trail of jackets and jeans and rags gone red, as always the morning after—the messy evidence of two lovers who shed their clothing before eating the other up.

I let the first bus pass, thinking myself early. Then

another and no old man, no sweet or sour. I took the third, and when I got to the school, I found chains cuffing the doors. I put my fist against the glass until the guard came out from behind the building, telling me that the day was canceled on account of last night and what would take place again and more so tonight and that it wasn't entirely safe, in his professional opinion, for me to be out on my own, and did I have someone to pick me up? I said, Don't be silly, but if it possibly wasn't entirely safe for me it might also possibly not be entirely safe for an old man, and I thought how he had always been as sure and steady as the downtown clock and what did he do and where did he go but outside to the people when the world terrified him?

DESPITE THE GUARD'S and the radioman's and the newspapers' suggestion for individuals to stay in their homes, I ventured out that evening. I had bought a new jacket, a burnt-orange number that would do well in the chill, and I wanted to show it off to the old man.

It was dark by the time I got downtown. Rounding a corner, I saw the people streaming into the square, the mass of them glowing with small fires carried in their hands. I joined the back where they kept the Sunday morning folks—old men and women, the youngest children. After reading so many reports, I felt the excitement that came when a beloved book was made into film, all of a sudden visible and real.

The old man was nowhere in sight. I worked my way up—small candles progressing in size and heat to beer bottles to liquor bottles to torches. I stopped one row behind the frontline, where a hot silence draped itself over the crowd. Peeking up on my toes, I fought for a view between shoulders. The people leaders had stopped before the men leaders, no more than a breath between them. The men in power had covered themselves in plastic: square black helmets with tinted visors over their faces and plates of protective rubber embedded in their uniforms. Each had tucked himself behind a shield with one shoulder, holding a black club or metal blade in the opposite hand.

A teenager with a blue bandana over his face whispered down to me, You shouldn't be up here.

It started the way anything started: with a seed of quaking static in your gut, a feeling like you're moving but not moving, and then a wild overflow, a purging, a getting the inside out as fast as possible.

A young man in front, looking at the men, cried out, Annie!

And the crowd behind him cried, Annie! Justice!

Betsy! he cried.

Betsy! Justice! the crowd responded.

Charlie!

Charlie! Justice!

Dante!

Dante! Justice! the crowd yelled.

And Eric, Frankie, and Geoffrey; Harry, Iona, and James on down the line, each response faster, each filled to the brim with heat—all the while, the uniforms hiding men motionless—Kathy, Larry, Michael, all the way to *P* for Peter. I didn't know how many Peters there were in the world, how many in our city, but in between the young man's saying it and the crowd's dutiful echo, I saw a particular Peter, a perfect whisper of a schoolboy, a pristine castrato who only ever sang the pains of boyhood into beauty, and after the crowd added *Justice*, I responded with a cry of my own, a sound that could have been the scream of a child or a mother losing that child, and the scene quickly became something confusing.

The back of the crowd surged, pushing the front of the line into the men, who pushed back with their plastic plates. They pushed and pushed until the line broke, the people and the men zipping themselves up, boy, man, boy, man, until there was no longer anything separating us. I saw one of the men's long blades bared then made to disappear inside a young one. From behind me, rocks and more rocks, bigger rocks, and flaming bottles took flight. I covered my head with my hands, trying to move out by moving back. I ducked and dipped, muscling through while making myself as small as possible. As I was nearly out, a shoulder knocked me to the ground, and down there with me was a body, a small body, which I put into my arms. I stood. I hunched and pushed, stepping on feet and hands. I got out of the crowd to the edge of the square, where the concrete fell away to hard dirt, and the dark trees of the park picked up. I got down on my knees, cradling the small body in the bowl of my lap. The body was a child, a breathing child I did not know or recognize. A boy or girl child, a cap of short black hair with a ring of oily red around its head, red that bled down the rest of its body, as a baby pushed from the womb, covered in the messy violence of its mother's flesh. I looked to the crowd for a mother or sister missing the child, but I saw only bodies, one against the other, and from inside the clash a man with a long blade breaking free. He moved toward me and the child, a confident march neither slow nor fast, the man as faceless and irrevocable as fear itself. The red was coming from inside the child's head and it shone all around its face. Its eyes were looking at me with so much blank hunger, like my eyes could feed his, hers, its chest's breaths winding down, and I said, You're beautiful. It's okay. You're beautiful. You're so beautiful; you look just like me.

GUN CONTROL

IF THERE'S A GUN IN ACT ONE, fire it in act three. Make it loud. Make it bang. Call it a climax.

If there's a gun in act one, fire it in act two. Let the rising and falling action make a perfect, even-sided triangle. Make it a cartoon mountain peak. Call it *isosceles*.

If there's a gun in act one, fire it in act one. We can see it there, we know what you want to do with it. There's no need to be coy.

If there's a gun in act one, push out the barrel and tip the bullets onto a quilt-covered bed in act one. The soft sound of their plunking. Guns are dangerous and more dangerous when the bullets are left inside.

Alternatively, if there's a gun in act one, keep the bullets inside it. Do not fire it in act one, two, or three. Guns are dangerous and more dangerous when the bullets are left inside.

If there's a gun in act one, describe the gun as cold. As smooth. Describe the gun as feeling heavier than it looks. Note the weight specifically. Compare it to something more familiar and innocuous. A wrench? A lead pipe? A bag with two or three apples inside it? Depending on the size of the apples.

If there's a gun in act one, put it in a fenced-in backyard. Let its shots in act one, act two, act three be an annoyance, as a neighbor's dog. Wonder why the dog won't stop barking. Wonder whether it is barking at anyone in particular. Think, Surely it will run out of barks soon.

If there's a gun in act one, have the dog bury it in the backyard in act two. Let the gun be a bone-dead thing we forget about and that decomposes, becomes part of the earth. Or let the gun be a seed that is watered and allowed to sprout and become tree and bear fruit that we may then pick and eat or can in jars to be placed in our cellar, lined up in rows against the wall for cold times, drought times, less plentiful gun times, so that we may never go without.

Or take the harvest to the farmers market to sell by

weight in green paper cartons, cheaper the more you buy, a half peck, full peck, bushel of guns.

If there's a gun in act one, let it instead be a banana. Let the hero slip on the peel, fall onto the third rail of the subway tracks in act two, and while he's being electrocuted, let the banana shoot him in the head.

If there's a gun in act one, flirt with it in act two. Treat it like a boy. Look at it, look away, then look back again. See the gun, but more important, let the gun see you. Know that the second time you look, you'd better be ready to put your finger on the gun's trigger and take the gun into your mouth as far as it will go because otherwise why did you look at the gun a second time?

If there's a gun in act one, in act two let the story of the gun become a will they/won't they.

The gun is in love with you or you with it or both of you in love with each other. But know that the thing you most want in this world—to be killed by the gun in act three—is never going to happen. The closest you'll get is a near miss. A graze of the temple, the crisp deletion of a pinky toe, a finger snipped off like someone clipping her nails. Know that the near miss will be followed by the gun's girlfriend or wife walking in and saying, What's going on here? Someone had better explain this. Know that, because you love the gun and don't want to get it into trouble, despite the gun's inherent danger, despite how close it came to killing you for nothing, you will have to lie for the gun. You will have to say, Blood? What blood? You will have to say, I was just playing with this . . . knife. I love knives. You will say, I really did think the safety was on.

Remember that counter to *if gun, then fire* runs the deeper, truer maxim that only unrequited love can be romantic. The gun must be away from us, unfired, incomplete, unsatisfied, in order to hold any kind of love potential. That's why we must keep the bullets inside.

Know that you may go through acts one, two, and three without ever having a gun, let alone the gun you love, fire a single bullet in your direction. This will create sympathy or its uglier, more honest cousin, pity, for you in your readers, though some, no matter how subtle your rendering of your unrequited love pain, will still think you're a sad sack who shouldn't be in love with a gun to begin with and certainly not a gun who already has a girlfriend.

And so if there's a gun in act one, put the gun to your temple in act one, finger smoothing the trigger, just to see how that feels. Just to see how you might act in subsequent acts. Just to see how one act might lead to another.

If there's a gun in act one, pry it out of your cold dead hand in act three, but not until late in the act when your hand will have clawed especially cold and especially dead around the gun. Snap your fingers off if need be. Let the story be about your hand not wanting to ever let go.

If there's a gun in act one, let act three be so far away that the gun rusts, jams, seizes, so that it's no more useful than a rock, which is similar in size and weight to a fist, the size and weight of a man's heart, which is a pretty good thing to kill someone with.

If there's a gun in act one, let its firing in act three become so inevitable as to become predictable. Let the inevitability become a hum over which the real story is laid, let the inevitability be like the dog's bark echoing throughout the neighborhood, but not close by, not even one door down, not so annoying and disruptive that you need to do something about the dog, not so disruptive that you need to *take care of* the dog, i.e., take the dog out of its yard in the middle of the night, drive it out of town, tie it to a tree, etc.

Despite knowing that *if gun, then fire*, despite knowing that it's not just inevitability but persistence, a kind of insistence, a drive and purpose like gravity, know that *if gun, then fire* will outlive you, know that *if gun, then fire* might even kill you. Nonetheless, grind your wheels, if only a little, against *if gun, then fire*. You might, for example, take the gun somewhere you've never been before in act two. You will have to drive or walk or bike (you cannot fly with a gun; they do not allow it in carry-ons and we don't have time for checking bags). For example, you might drive or walk as far east as you can go. Which means, eventually, depending on where act one begins, hitting a mountain, an ocean, a cliff. Take the gun, and assuming it's still a gun, throw it as far as you can throw it. Loosen up your arm, rear back, make it a good one. Keep the bullets inside it. At the edge of the water or cliff, the top of the mountain, the bubbling mouth of the volcano, you may see others doing or just having done the same thing. Give a nod, perhaps even do a secret hand signal—a tug of the ear, a swipe of the nose—but say nothing. Do not smile. Do not congratulate yourself or the others for the long journey to the gun's obliteration. This is something you and the others should have done a long time ago, long before act one even began.

If the gun in act one has become a banana in act two, let the gun, instead, be a banana clip. Something plastic, built to break, something that went out of style in the mid-nineties. Something that people now only wear ironically. And so let the banana clip be a kind of joke that cannot hold up to the weight of scrutiny, the roll of our collective eyes.

If there's a gun in act one, and in act two or three the gun is no longer a gun, then fire it—that is, discharge it—for not holding up its end of the bargain.

If in act one the gun has become a banana, use the banana to kill as many children in the school as possible. Show up hours or days or weeks in advance and plant the banana and dozens of other bananas in hidden corners of the school, where they will eventually (at some point in the now distant-seeming act three) rot and cause a horrible smell to disseminate throughout the school, thick as smoke, sending the teachers and children and lunch workers pouring out of the building like vital fluid from a wound, pinching their noses or the noses of their friends.

Give the parents, the teachers, perhaps even one child the chance to say, We were supposed to be having our science fair today. It was such a fun, exciting thing we were going to do. But now this. I guess we'll have to have the science fair tomorrow or the next day. We'll just come back tomorrow.

If this, then end the story now, leave the children looking ahead to, but not quite getting, the science fair. This will put them in a state of insecurity (What if the same thing happens tomorrow? What if there are more bananas?) but also of hope, which is a good state in which to leave things—that is to say complicated, perhaps only slightly wiser, potentially, probably a little sadder than before.

But if you'd like to raise the stakes, if you'd really like to make the story worth telling, send one kid to the emergency room because they thought he was having an allergic reaction to the bananas. Instead have it turn out that he had begun hyperventilating on account of pinching his nose too tightly. Let it be a mistake. Let it just be that everyone is overreacting to the incident with the bananas.

If the gun in act one has become a banana in act two, keep one banana—a last-resort banana—tucked into the back of your jeans with your shirt pulled over top. When all the other bananas have spoiled, have split their soft guts onto the floor, peel the banana, put your finger on the trigger of the banana, and force the remaining children and teachers closest to you to each take a bite. They might turn their heads or even begin to cry for the awkwardness of something shoved into their mouths, but just do it. Bananas are for eating, and so make them take as many bites as they can, but, and this is important, be sure to save the last bite for yourself. It is, after all, your banana.

In order to erase ourselves in act one or two or three, to make disappear the men behind the gun, if there's a gun in act one, give everyone a gun in act one. Let it be assumed that all men and women are gunned, holding, packing. So in act three when guns are drawn, yours pointing at his, his pointing at hers, hers pointing at hers at yours, it will be no surprise. It will be a given that those guns were there all along, and so *if gun, then fire* will serve as a least common denominator for our stories, the point from which we start all stories, as language, as body, as breath, as the clearing of a throat just before speech.

Because it will sometimes be satisfying for people to say, Yes, he was always strange. Always standoffish. Antisocial. He always was. For them to say, His family always did love bananas.

It will also be satisfying to say the opposite. To insert, despite *If gun act one, then fire act three*, the baffled character of ourselves, the tortured mother, the ravaged sister survivor standing in the parking lot, saying, I never in a million years. I had no idea. You just cannot predict something like this.

WINE IS
MOSTLY WATER

THEY PUSH HOOKS THROUGH the man's calves, back, and arms and hang him from the gallery ceiling. Skin pulled to points, skin stretched like bats' wings. It's called the Superman pose: facedown, body spread out thirty feet in the air. Adam doesn't understand the physics of it, why his skin doesn't tear, though he knows it has to do with the number of hooks. In this pose, he needs eight. Guy, the man who suspends him, says that some people in different poses can get away with only two; it all depends on their skin.

Adam wears nothing but a pair of nylon shorts. They match his pale coloring, so that at first glance he appears naked, and then, on longer inspection, naked still, a eunuch. The shorts itch when he puts them on, but like the hooks, if he doesn't move, he feels them less and less until he stops feeling them at all. He instead feels the air around him, how far he is from the gallery floor and the people standing below. At his younger sister's studio apartment, the coffee table is inches from the couch he sleeps on. The arm of the couch is inches from her bed pillow. Some nights, he puts his head at the couch's arm, some nights his feet. Other nights she asks that he not come home so she can have the apartment to herself.

The exhibit is, in some ways, about flight, about putting impossible objects in the air. In the first room, a glass of water hovers just inches off the floor. It's hard to tell immediately that it's not flush to the ground. A placard on the wall asks that viewers not touch any part of the installation, but they cannot help bending down and waving their hands around the glass. It looks so much like magic.

As the exhibit progresses, the objects get higher and higher. Two books, splayed open, float hip-high. A dark-wood bedside table comes to viewers' necks. The contents of its open drawer are visible to most only when they balance on their toes: a handful of gray-wrapped condoms, pencils, and a steno tablet filled with scrawl.

A tall brass lamp hovers some feet away and higher, lit and cocked at an angle. Viewers step around its shadow, the place where it would fall were it to fall. Then, walking through a narrow hallway, instinctively looking up one increment higher, they enter the other room. There a bed hovers upside down, pillows secured to its head, but blankets and sheets left to hang, as if to say that this is not solely about defying gravity. Then a scattering of clothes—a black bra, a balled white sock, a pair of cotton underwear. The loose parabola at once leads up to and trails away from Adam, as rock and fire and dust pulled behind a dying comet. It's hot near the ceiling. Alex, the exhibit's creator, told him to expect this, but each night it surprises him how surely the heat comes into his body. One moment the temperature is an antiseptic cool, the next his skin flushes, the feeling bleeding out from his chest like a stain. The problem is not the heat or being so far off the ground or the numbing pain that leaves him feeling both within and outside his body. It's coming down, it's being released. It's the phantom cords tugging him backward as he walks to his sister's home.

LAST WEEK HE FLEW HOME to visit his father in Fort Wayne. The temperature had reached ninety before noon, and the house Adam grew up in, a gray foursquare on the south side of town, is still without air-conditioning. He had gotten comfortable on the porch swing with a book on the seventeen-year cicada and a glass of iced tea when his father came out and handed him a letter. He sat down across from Adam in an Adirondack chair, and as Adam was finishing reading, his father eased down beside him gingerly, as though trying not to wake a sleeping baby.

He isn't his father, the letter told him. His mother not his mother and sister Sandy not his sister Sandy. The handwriting was neat and slanted forward, a tidy brick of text. But I love you very much and always will, it said.

His father was just inches away from him, hands stuffed in between his thighs, the two of them pushing the swing with their feet. Strange, Adam thought, the swing's movement accompanying such a letter, as though everything should have stopped upon his reading it.

Why are you telling me this? he asked finally.

Your mother hadn't wanted to tell you. When she got sick—even then she didn't want to tell you. His father coughed.

It had been over two years since his mother died, and it was unsettling to think of his father defying some wish of hers, that there were secrets she thought she was taking with her. This, he realized, was more surprising than his father not being his father—a friendly, sometimes bumbling man who couldn't offend or be offended

by anyone. A man who conjured in Adam a guilty embarrassment, with his midwestern naïveté and optimism.
Adam had always been more like his mother. Singular,
sardonic, independent. Both he and Sandy. But his
mother's hair, her dark wiry hair and high cheekbones,
were not his, and he sensed the blossoming magnolias in
the yard twisting away from him, sliding along some invisible track, as though rigged pieces of a theater set
being pulled offstage.

But Sandy's not adopted, Adam said. How had his
father put it? *While Sandy was birthed of your mother.*

No, it turns out, how shall I put this, our *productivity*
problems weren't such problems after all.

And you don't know who these *donors* were?

No, they chose to stay anonymous. Healthy, though.
Young. Unfortunately they don't have all the informa
tion they do now—IQ, favorite color, all that. His father
pushed his wire glasses up his nose.

Does Sandy know?

I was going to speak with her after I talked to you.
Unless you'd like to have that conversation with your
sister?

A year ago, the graphic design firm he'd been working for let Adam go. Six months after that, he shed three-
quarters of his belongings and moved into his sister's
studio. When he's not at the gallery, he makes them
dinner. Pasta, big salads, omelets. Afterward they read

or watch a movie on his laptop, the two of them smashed together on the couch like children who never left their parents' home.

A little help here, son? his father said. Adam had stopped pushing and the swing was moving unevenly. He righted it with his foot, wanting to yell at his father. He knew how easy it would be to make him feel bad, that he wouldn't defend himself. Instead, he would bumble. He would say, Well, I-I'm *sorry*—the soft skin of his jowls shaking—and there would be nothing satisfying in it.

They spent the rest of the day on the porch, talking slowly about nothing. Adam's father would go inside to refill their iced tea and Adam would note the difference on the swing with the weight of his father gone. He would reemerge from the house carrying a plate of apples and cheese or boiled hot dogs with a palette of condiments. Once, sitting beside him again, his father pointed to a cluster of hostas in the yard, bursting with growth, and said, Adam, look. Last week, they were only *this* big.

ADAM WATCHES SANDY get ready for work. He's on the couch in a pair of shorts; she's standing outside the bathroom, tucking a silk blouse into a gray pencil skirt. Face hard and staring at nothing. No one would guess they aren't related. If not siblings, then at least cousins. His hair is similarly dark, skin similarly pale, a resemblance that has only increased with age, as though they were growing into each other, as friends or lovers dress or talk alike over time.

Sandy disappears into the bathroom then reemerges, shaking her wet hair. Her movements—bending to pick up a sock or square a stack of books—have been so uncannily *Sandy* it feels like watching an actress who has studied her for years, combed her hair just so, and taken her place. The woman is talented, so assured in her role that even her slips into melodrama feel like Sandy, if not *more* Sandy. Fast-walking, focused Sandy. It all appears unsettlingly right, as when a liar moves so deeply into his lie that he convinces himself it's true.

Has Dad talked to you lately? Adam asks.

No, why? She's pouring milk over a bowl of cereal at the kitchen counter.

Not since I've been back?

She brings her bowl and mug to the couch, stepping over Adam's shoes and backpack. Scooch, she says, and Adam turns forward. *Scooch*—how many times has he heard that from her?

Nothing?

The last time we talked he was going on about how hot this summer was and how I haven't been out there in a while. Why, is he mad at me?

He's not *mad*.

What is he then?

He thinks about his father on the swing, his skinny legs poking out from his khaki shorts, the way he'd served Adam ice cream with Grape-Nuts on top, like he had when they were kids.

He's nothing. He's fine.

Have you been losing weight? Sandy pinches the side of his bare stomach.

He flinches. He has always been a slender man—a certain body type, Guy has told him, is necessary for suspension—but it's true, there seems to be less of him.

I sweat buckets up there.

Does it ever fall on people?

I don't know, he says. Sometimes he thinks about spitting on them. He imagines them pretending to know what it all means and wanting to deflate their pretension. But the thought occurs the way a smoker long since having quit considers a cigarette—the desire rises then disappears almost at once. It's no longer me, he thinks, with neither pleasure nor sadness. He considers himself from a dull distance.

Anyway, he says, Alex hasn't said anything. But she's not really there.

I thought Alex was a man.

Nope.

Ah, *now* it all makes sense.

What?

Those nude shorts, she says. She's one of your girls.

It has always bothered Adam the way Sandy ribs him about women. When he lived alone and would meet up with Sandy for a drink, it wasn't uncommon for them to run into girls he'd been dating. Slender girls with tall, pointed shoes who worked in PR or marketing, sexy assistant positions seemingly only filled with girls like this. Girls with straight hair and slick, confident intelligence. He'd see them for three weeks, two months, and grow heavy with their want, the way he could see them trying to please him. Once, one of those girls found him and Sandy at a bar downtown. A girl with dark tights disappearing into black ankle boots and a leather clutch in her hand. Thinking Sandy was a new girlfriend, she said, He's a roamer, he gets bored. Believe me. Before Adam could respond—a beat to remember her name—the woman slid herself back into the crowd like a pickpocket. With a raised eyebrow, Sandy said, You never told me about that one. His sister's comment bothers him more now that he doesn't go out like he used to.

When Adam first met Alex to discuss the exhibit, she'd started out all business. In a white, windowless office in the back of the gallery, an empty desk and a cluster of microphone stands in the corner, she had him take off his shirt. She stood, arms crossed, viewing him like something she had made. Her dark blonde hair was dry and wavy down her back, and a thick set of bangs hung over her eyes. Her oxford shirt with the sleeves rolled up and loose jeans made her seem at once masculine and smaller, hidden.

This is so objectifying, she said, shaking her head, eyes dazed. She began nodding. It's awesome. You're really attractive. Oh, I probably shouldn't say that. She slapped her hand over her mouth, pretending to laugh.

Adam found her at once endearing and off-putting—immediately familiar with him but not secure in that familiarity. He decided to play along. Dressing, he asked, So, does that mean I get the job? But her phone rang just then. She took it from her pocket, looked at its screen, then silenced it.

I think I'm going to commit *suicide*, she said, all the playfulness drained from her face. He must have given her a look, because she snorted and said, Jeez, just kidding. Later as he was leaving, he saw her outside crying into her phone with all the red, open force of a teenager: I *am* trying to deal with it!

Adam had ducked his head and sped past her to the subway.

Opening night, suspended, he had watched her walk the circle of the gallery. She drank wine, shook people's hands, but she often stood to the side playing with her phone or straightening the exhibit cards on the entrance table. Her short, compact body swam within long layers of gray and brown wool, looking like she'd draped an old tablecloth over her shoulders. She projected a distinctly keyed-up energy from some edge that he couldn't see. It both intrigued and annoyed him.

I don't have any girls, Adam says. Anyway she's weird.

I'll have to see her first.

When are you coming down?

Closing night, she says. When it's all over.

THAT EVENING BEFORE OPENING, Alex goes up with Adam on the lift to watch Guy suspend him.

I feel like I should see how it's done, she says.

You gonna stick around for the show? Adam asks.

Sure, she replies, with too much energy.

The platform is no bigger than a closet and Adam, belly down, rests his chin on his folded arms, the metal of the lift cool against his skin. Alex sits on one side of him; on the other Guy dots Adam's back with a marker. Guy has dark hair and thick arms. He wears jeans and a black T-shirt every day like a uniform, working with the silent efficiency of a tailor or barber.

The holes from last week closed up, he says. I'm going to go just to the side of them . . .

Adam feels a hand run the length of his back, fingering the skin where the hooks will go. It isn't until Guy stands and cracks his neck that he realizes the hand belongs to Alex.

Sort of makes you wonder what everyone's like at home, she says.

When Guy doesn't answer, Adam turns his head: Were you talking to me?

Whoever, she says shrugging. She speaks with so much forced casualness, he thinks, as though every possible response were exactly what she expected. She thumbs the elastic at his waist, sending a creeping tickle up to his neck.

Have you lost weight? she asks. Don't get all anorexic on me.

Happens all the time to people who suspend this much, Guy says. He's back down kneeling. Here's a sting, he says, and with a small piercing gun, he punches a hole through the skin below Adam's right shoulder, following it with a hook at the end of a cable.

I haven't been doing it for that long.

Though wouldn't that be a project? Alex asks. Taking pictures of a fat man getting skinny? You're not fat, but it'd be very dramatic. And then by the end you'd become way too skinny, and then we'd realize that maybe you didn't want to lose all that weight?

Guy clears his throat. Here's another sting, he says.

What do you think, Adam, she asks. Do you want to be my way-too-skinny?

Sure.

I'm just kidding. I'd never want you to do that to yourself. This skinniness is too much. You'd look better with a few extra pounds.

You'd look better with a few less.

Guy snorts. Adam's back shifts, quivering like the flanks of a horse. This used to come naturally. Handing out insults to see how people would react. Now it feels like someone he no longer likes hanging around uninvited.

I'm not saying you're fat. You're very petite, he says, but you wouldn't know it to look at you. You're wearing too many clothes. You've got to be baking. Am I right? He turns back to look at Guy. He's on his feet, untwirling another cord from the frame in the ceiling.

It's wicked hot out, Guy replies, not taking his eyes off his work. He kneels down and, with the gun, places the last hook and cable. He looks at his watch and says, All right, we better do this. Guy takes another, thicker cord running down from the pulley above the frame. He pulls slowly. Adam's skin lifts away from his body, then his body lifts away from the platform. Guy raises him to head height.

Alex stands before him. Her face has gone flat, eyes dulled. That old satisfaction pulses in Adam, the one that comes from finding out exactly how much someone will put up with.

How does it feel? she asks.

Like my skin is being ripped off, Adam laughs.

Alex smirks. That's a shame.

ADAM DRESSES IN THE OFFICE at the end of the night. There's a voicemail from his sister asking that he not come home, saying that she'll buy him dinner later in the week to make up for it. Her voice comes to him from a strict distance. The objects in the room shift toward then away from him, as when he finished reading his father's letter. The porch, the plants, the trees all converged into one point, curving and stretching from one place to another while remaining static, unmistakably the same. The man his sister is bringing home for the night is faceless, nobody Adam knows. She won't tell him who this man is nor will he ask.

He finds Alex rinsing out a wineglass in the kitchenette across from the office.

You're here late.

Oh, she says, turning to face him. Yeah, just cleaning up.

They have people to do that, you know.

I know. She puts a hand behind her on the counter, the other at her hip, a pose just awkward enough for

Adam to notice. She sighs and crosses her arms. Would you like to get a drink? she asks.

Sure.

Where should we go?

How about your place?

She drops her head into her chest, then raises it. Her cheeks have gone red, but her smile is slow and controlled. All right, she says.

You're blushing.

THEY TAKE THE TRAIN to Alex's neighborhood and cut through the park. Twenty years ago, the place was filled with needles and bums and drug dealers in hooded sweatshirts. Now there are couples with strollers and a group of twentysomethings throwing a Frisbee.

I chose you for a reason, you know, Alex says.

Because I'm not too skinny.

No, she says. Well, partly you were the right body type, but mostly it was your face. Your features are classic. Like an old movie star. No one famous, though. No one recognizable.

I see.

I wanted people to be able to project onto you whoever they wanted.

The distance helps.

Of course, but still.

Who are you projecting onto me?

She looks away and back. Isn't it obvious? she says, her voice sad yet reprimanding.

Her loft is at least four times the size of his sister's place—airy and open. The apartment's lights and the fuzzed shapes of their bodies reflect back at them in the tall glass windows. Before them sits a long, sleek couch with a stack of folded blankets and pillows in white cases. It takes Adam a minute to realize what's missing.

Don't you have a bed?

It's in the gallery, she says, from the kitchen, uncorking a bottle.

You're kidding.

No, it's all actually mine. And his. Our broken bedroom.

That's a little over-the-top, don't you think?

She approaches, carrying two glasses of red wine out ahead of her body.

That's the point, she says, handing him a glass.

He follows her to the couch. She turns her glass slowly in her lap, a wave of quiet moving over her. Her sadness is plain and bare and Adam can't decide whether or not he wants to see it.

It's funny, she says, her face moving closer to the one she uses in the gallery. Seeing you half-naked all these nights, I kind of like you better in your clothes. He is, like Guy, wearing slim jeans, a black T-shirt, and black canvas shoes.

I guess I'll just keep them on then, he says, smiling.

Don't be ridiculous.

They move from the couch to the floor, laying out blankets and using pillows. She looks small naked. He feels like a blade trying to whittle her soft body down even smaller. They turn each other over, say, How about this? Let's try this on. Then: Put your leg here. No, here. He pulls her hair, digs his thumbs deep into her forearms. She curls her body into his hands. It's the way she dresses—sloppy, her body an afterthought—he knows he can do anything with her.

Adam will not remember who, but somewhere in the heated middle, one of them will say, I love you. So much. And the other will reply, I love you too. So fast, it will feel simultaneous, slowing nothing down to say it. They keep on until they grow bored and tired and there's nothing left for them to do but crawl up onto the long, thin couch and try to claim a spot as their own.

THE BRIGHT MORNING LIGHT pushes through the apartment's tall windows. Alex sits up on the opposite end of the couch, rolling her neck. Adam doesn't realize how much makeup she wears until now, until there is none. She looks washed-out and faded, and he feels oddly reassured that she isn't more vain, isn't one of those women who won't let men see them without makeup. She regards him for a moment, as though an object that used to hold meaning for her but no longer does. He has the sudden desire to hold her hand—this open, blank sadness so real that he wants to touch it.

She disappears into the bathroom then pads into the kitchen, wearing a tank top and a pair of white underwear, loose around her hips.

It's not until the teakettle builds to a howl that he remembers, as if recalling a dream, what they said the night before. He watches her pour the water into a French press at the kitchen counter, the steam, for a moment, masking her face.

She brings him his coffee in a white mug and sits beside him, folding her legs beneath her. Adam used to grow annoyed with too much morning-after chatter, but the silence feels expectant, like he's been asked a question but can't remember it.

I'm adopted, he says.

Oh, I didn't know that.

I didn't know. I found out a couple weeks ago. My dad told me.

Just now? She sips from her mug. How do you feel about it?

I don't know. The weird thing is my sister doesn't know. My dad didn't tell her.

Are you going to tell her?

I don't know.

She purses her lips and says, I don't understand that kind of indecision.

Why complicate things?

I don't know, so you can have an honest relationship? Her face is guileless. It makes her look younger, the strain of her everything-is-easy persona now shed, as though she had also disclosed a secret.

You think you're always honest with people?

I don't lie, she shrugs.

That's not the same thing.

Still, I don't lie.

Never? He's almost laughing now.

I might question later whether or not I actually believed something when I felt it, but I always believe things when I say them. Why pretend?

You're so weird.

I know! She smiles and it grows deeply into her face.

He puts his hand on her thigh.

WHEN ADAM RETURNS HOME, his sister is smoking in the armchair at the foot of her bed, knees to chest, hair in a loose mass atop her head.

Aren't you supposed to be at work? he says.

I took a sick day.

Adam looks at her bed, stripped of its sheets, the comforter crumpled on the floor.

Everything okay?

Fine.

You sure?

She nods.

You seem a little—

I'm fine, really. Her voice is calm but firm, her face clean of emotion.

You have a cut, he says, stepping closer, putting a finger to his cheek.

There's a red line within the half circle of skin beneath her eye. She turns and exhales her smoke toward the window behind her, the sun coming in white-hot.

Sandy, did you hear me? He stops just next to the chair, letting his thigh lean onto the arm. There's a little red—

She turns back, looking straight at him. Adam, there's a little red all up and down your back. And your legs and your arms. It's all crusty and pus.

Well, you know what that's from.

It's disgusting.

She gives him a sardonic, distanced smile. Sometimes she meets up with a woman from work, for drinks or dinner, or treats herself to a movie, but every couple

of months she goes out on a bender. She winds up drinking too much and yelling at someone or blacking out and
not remembering a thing. She used to call Adam the
next day crying, embarrassed and depressed. She'd say
things like, I've just been having such a hard time lately,
My life is a mess. She rarely went into detail. He imagines her sitting alone in the apartment, drinking a bottle
of wine and falling asleep. Cutting herself. He sees an
alternate, fuller story to the one she gives. A smile creeps
onto her face.

Where'd you stay last night?

SANDY ARRIVES HALFWAY THROUGH the final night.
Her pace is slow and intentional. He would recognize her
on the other side of a wall, Adam thinks. She gives him a
discreet, hip-high wave when she first looks up, then
continues her circle around the room's perimeter. She
finds Alex almost immediately. They shake hands and
stand awkwardly apart—Sandy's body erect yet contained, Alex hunched and folded in.

He has liked being a part of Alex's design, but probably not as much as she has enjoyed having him there.
An attractive man strung up for her vision, her pleasure.
Next week, she'll take the pieces down one at a time and
have them delivered to her loft, but it won't be as easy to
fit them back in as it was to take them out.

As in weeks past, Adam's initial pain from the cables changes into a pressurized weightlessness. The sound below downshifts to an abstract hum. Adam sees his body as hairless, slowly moving away from him. He thinks of an exhibit in which a man gets smaller and smaller. Except it's a man and then a young man and then a boy. Somewhere there is a man and a woman, together or separate, blocks or miles away from Adam's father's house in Fort Wayne. People who might think of Adam, a nameless man and woman just as Adam is nameless to them. A man, maybe only a woman, who said, I will not be tied to another. I will commit to no life, not even my own. Adam was just out of school when he started at the graphic design firm. He did good work, went out every night. He'd joke with his coworkers and call all the girls sluts and the guys lame and dickless. Years this way, feeling as though he were skating above people—small people—dropping down like a seabird to pierce a fish, having a good time until the girl he was into told him that he was an asshole and a punk, that no one thought he was funny or clever or talented. She'd delivered to him a controlled, angry monologue. He started going out less and less, and when he did, he'd talk slowly out of the side of his mouth. Then he lost his job and moved in with Sandy. He thinks about it sometimes, how he used to be a completely different person.

The crowd thins and vanishes. The lights reflect off

the blond-wood floor in fuzzed circles Adam can hear the mechanical echo of the lift from a far corner of the gallery. It inches into view, with Guy behind its tiny black wheel. After tonight he will have to find something to do with himself, maybe pick up some freelance work. He should find a job like Guy's. An occupation that means nothing more than what it shows itself to be. A driver, a housepainter, a clerk. He should move heavy objects from one place to another, wear a uniform. Alex and Sandy stand just below Adam, their voices shooting up before dropping back down to the close talk of conspirators. They step out of the way as Guy parks the lift before them. Sandy tilts her head down toward Alex, who is whispering something into her ear. Their sharp laughter rises to meet him, cracking like a firework before dissolving into an echoey silence. Then, as if they planned it all along, as if sisters who've spent their lives finishing each other's sentences, they call up to him: Time to come down.

DANNY GIRL

ANNY IS UPSTAIRS in her father's house throwing herself around. She falls on the gray-white futon, rolls, and gets up, breathless. Her shirt's off. Her breasts are nubs. The room, halved by stairs, holds a twin bed covered in an afghan on one side, the dirty futon on the other. The wood beams of the sloped roof are bare, and cobwebs palm their corners. Last weekend Danny saw a movie where a couple was fighting; then they kissed. They kept kissing and were still angry. Danny is fighting with a boy man. Then she is the boy-man, shirtless, straight jeans at her hips. Next she's a cowboy wrestling a calf; then she is herself again, surprised and violated by the boy.

Her father is downstairs, her sisters and stepmother and stepbrothers too. On the weekends, they form a loose, shifting mass. Each sits or lies or sleeps away from the other, spread out like jacks. The wood-burning stove heats the living room too hot, though upstairs Danny can feel the wind, thin and cold, coming through the walls. She is panting, working herself into a feeling. She smells her own sweat and a new, deeper fetor, that salty, sour smell of the school locker room, where last week a pair of girls said she should start wearing a bra—two girls, one tall and rail-thin with bug eyes, and the other with blonde, fluffy bangs and breasts that she presses out with an arch in her back. You need to wear a bra, the blonde one said, just like that.

When Danny finishes, she puts on her shirt and goes downstairs. In the parlor beside the living room stands a wooden bar, hulking and lacquered, and across from it the black stove. All day it smells of woodsmoke. Danny's mother told her and her sisters that their father was an idiot for the stove, that all it does is make the rest of a house colder and angry that it doesn't get the same heat as the other rooms but that it'll get sick of the hot rooms eventually too. Danny's mother had said this in the kitchen, clicking her fingernails on the countertop in dumb Morse code.

But he can do whatever he wants, she said. He can do whatever *he* wants, and we can do whatever *we* want—right, ladies? she said, raising a glass of pink drink to the three of them. Danny's younger sister had used both hands to put her sippy cup into the air. Danny is thirsty; it is so warm near the stove. She walks into the living room, where on the television a white-blonde-haired girl is whispering into the ear of an old man in striped pajamas. Lying in a bed, he makes his face big, his eyes wide; he is shocked or pretending to be shocked over what the girl is telling him. Danny cannot hear what she says, the girl's lips curling slyly as she whispers; the words don't matter as much as her sneaking mouth. Her nonsense sibilants tickle Danny's ears, running down her neck and back, and now the man is playfully reprimanding the white-haired girl, talking to her like a teacher making an example. Then the girl is skipping down a sunny sidewalk in a mass of other girls, arms linked, their faces stretched out in rubbery laughter.

Danny's father and stepmother are on the couch, but Danny cannot see them. They're grayed out, smudged, as when a woman takes her top off on TV. Her father smokes all day, and the smoke drapes a curtain around him, the air heavy as velvet. Under the blast of television girls, Danny says she's hungry, and then there is money in her hand, and she and her sisters and stepbrothers are running across the road to the twenty-four-hour gas station, where they buy sour gummy slugs and deep-fried hot dog buns and burst jelly donuts. They return and divide everything up in the hot space behind the bar, where there are no bottles, only paper and pens and old magazines and jars of change, from which the sisters have fished out the silver-colored coins. They eat, kneeling, and when the youngest starts to cry, Danny's older sister gives her more sour slugs, and she shoves them into her wet mouth by the fistful. From the television, Danny hears a girl or woman curse, spitting the words out breathlessly, as though she'd just finished running.

AT HER MOTHER'S HOUSE, Danny gets a letter in the mail from her old classmate Margaret. Margaret tells her that it has been hard adjusting to the new town where she and her family moved last summer. The girls at school don't talk to her, she says. The school is bigger than she's used to. Margaret has a twin brother, and when she wore his clothes—velour shirts in anemic browns and navy-blue tennis shoes with Velcro straps— she became a lanky, slouching boy. Her hair formed the dirty top of a mushroom, and she talked slowly out of the side of her mouth like it had been numbed.

Margaret wishes she could come back. *You're my best friend,* she says. *Am I your best friend?* Danny used to get excited for the letters. She never gets mail. Now she gets annoyed. She can feel Margaret asking her to feel bad for her, wanting it too plainly. Danny hardens against the want, refusing to feel sorry for Margaret, but then feels bad for not feeling sorry, then feels angry that Margaret made her feel that way, and a different, twisted feeling stands up and falls down inside her stomach. Margaret says maybe Danny could visit her some weekend. It's only five hours away, she says. Could her mother drive her? *Please write back soon, even a postcard.* Danny puts the letter in a shoebox under her bed.

THE NEXT WEEKEND, Danny follows her stepbrother into the crawl space off his room. Leave a crack, he says, and she pulls the door closed behind her without shutting it all the way, as the handle is on the outside. The space is wedged beneath the sloped ceiling and has the same unfinished walls as the rest of the upstairs. Danny sometimes dreams that something bad, a faceless person or thing, is coming to the house and everyone needs to hide. There is very little time. Her sisters and stepbrothers and dad and stepmother all hide elsewhere, and she hides there, inside that tiny room, closing the door all the way shut then piling garbage bags of old underwear and bras on top of her. The dream ends with the thing opening the door, a blade of light cutting into the small, dark space.

The walls are covered with pictures of naked women ripped from magazines—their hair blonde and feathered, their genitals fleshy and blank. Danny pretends she cannot see them then stares. Their eyes are sleepy. Their mouths coo the O lip shape of babies who've just had their pacifiers tugged out. Everything is soft.

Where'd you get these pictures? Danny asks.

Daddy, her stepbrother says, but Danny doesn't know if he's talking about her dad or his. Cardboard boxes crowd behind him, some tops flapped open in flat shrugs. Sitting cross-legged, he lights a fat candle between the two of them. He pulls out a red bottle of cologne from the back of his jeans. It's Danny's father's.

Watch it, he says, and sprays a long pump into the candle, the flame whooshing large, licking Danny's knee, then disappearing. She scoots back.

The power is mine. Eat my fire, he says, mimicking a superhero with round, rubbery muscles and small candy-red underwear. The cologne smells rotten and sweet. He sprays it again. With each flame's breath, Danny's chest flares then cools, the paper women on the wall rising and falling with soft sighs. The cologne darkens a small, damp circle around the base of the candle like a sweat stain.

Her stepbrother moves the candle aside and takes out his small gray tape recorder and slides one of his tapes in. It's a bunch of songs from a cartoon full of cussing that he and his brothers watch. The first song is the cartoon people singing a cover with the words changed. The song bounces and turns and stretches. It's a funny song, and Danny smiles when her stepbrother begins to squeal with laughter, the song's plasticity unhinging her stomach. The troublemaker character buzzes in one ear then the other, delivering his defiant catchphrase, a chaotic hammering of short, blunt words. It makes her think that the world could turn upside down at any moment, and the cartoon character would think it was all a game. When the tape grinds then clicks to silence, her stepbrother sighs and looks up at the pictures on the wall, then he looks at Danny's chest—dull-eyed, his white-blond hair buzzed into a square, his face infested with freckles. He stares, and Danny feels hot and hushed, as she did the other day with the girls in the locker room. There was nothing to do but stay very quiet.

THE WEEK BEFORE Margaret's family left town, Margaret's mother had brought her over to see Danny. A bright, summer Saturday. The two of them had gone into Danny's mother's bedroom and sat on the bed—a slice of light coming through the window around the drawn shades. Danny had wanted to go outside. She never went into her mother's bedroom during the day, only sometimes at night when she couldn't sleep. Danny's legs dangled off the side of the bed, almost touching the floor. Margaret told Danny that her family was leaving because Margaret's father was bad. He had shown her a video. He had taken her into a bedroom just the two of them and sat her next to him on the bed and watched the video. He did not touch me, Margaret said, but he sat her beside him and he snorted drugs while they watched. Danny likes to forget the story. She likes to forget the story, and she thinks that Margaret likes to forget particular pieces of the story. It's only reasonable, Danny thinks. But Margaret's letters remind her. Danny had listened to Margaret's story silently, the two of them sitting on the bed's edge, Danny looking down at Margaret's Velcro shoes. Danny kept her hands folded neatly in her lap, thinking, This is a very adult conversation we're having.

WHEN HER HAIR COMES IN, Danny takes her father's electric razor and, sitting on the toilet in the downstairs bathroom, gets rid of it all. The razor crunches, her mouse-brown hairs falling light as ash into the bowl to rest on the water's surface. She blows the hair crumbs out of the razor's foil. She is so smooth. She pets herself, closing her eyes, tired. The bathroom, just off the kitchen, is cool, and she thinks about taking a bath, when there is a bang on the door.

What the hell are you doing in there? Son of a bitch, her father says.

Danny can hear the wet cigar wedged in the crook of his mouth. She flushes the toilet, pulls up her pants, and unplugs the razor, stuffing it in the cabinet under the sink. Danny opens the door, but her father is gone. There is only a pot of sauce on the stove, spitting red on the white walls. Her jeans rub her differently now. She walks upstairs into the second floor's coolness, then down into the parlor's heat. Up and down again. As hot as a stripped wire, her mother would say. Or, Ooh la la. Or, like the time her older sister rubbed lipstick on before school, Look at this hot bitch! Her sister had then erased it with her shirtsleeve.

The following week, Danny's hair comes back itchy, poking out straight through her underwear. Son of a bitch, she hisses. She scratches herself, leaving red fingernail tracks amid bumps and ingrown hairs. She squeezes one until glue-colored pus pops out. Son of a bitch.

MARGARET HAS A SURPRISE. She has a surprise, but first she has to tell Danny the whole situation. Margaret says the walk home from school has been longer than it was at home, which at first was really annoying. *It was so annoying I could not even believe it!* Her mom can't drive her because she has to take her younger sister, Elle, to ballet after school. Elle, a yellow-haired pixie, once told Danny that the freckle above her lip was not a freckle as Danny had said but a "beauty mark." Danny never believed she and Margaret were really sisters. Margaret's mom calls Elle the prima ballerina, Margaret says. *Whatever that means. But anyway,* the only thing that makes the walk better is that there's a boy, an older boy who is not in school anymore who talks to her on her walk. He drives a car, she says, and sometimes he drives it alongside her, but the last time, he parked and walked next to her. *Do you want to know what we talk about? I'll tell you if you want. Just write back and ask.* Danny rolls her eyes and puts the letter in her box.

DANNY SHOWERS in the upstairs stall, even though it is cold. She feels closed up inside it, as in a spaceship or submarine. The light is dim, the walls a textured plastic— small, raised bumps that she pretends are diseased skin. At her mother's, she stays in the bath for hours, topping the tub off with steaming water that weights her head so heavy that she pretends she's been drugged. She swirls her hair out in the water and pretends she's a sad woman or a dead girl in a movie. Sometimes she falls asleep and wakes up in the cold water and pretends she's a crazy woman, shivering uncontrollably. Eventually her mother will tap on the door, open it one shy creak at a time, then come in and sit on the toilet. Danny will add more water and bath syrup and cover herself with the bubbles. I'm bored, her mother will say. Your little sis is sleeping and your older sis is reading and *will not be disturbed*, and I have no one to talk to. Danny will emerge and sit in her terry robe and listen while her mother asks that she suggest to Danny's father that she's been spending a lot of special time with so-and-so from the such-and-such. The hunky one with the big boots, she'll say. Real big boots. Danny will only pretend to listen. Instead she will think of a boy, a faceless boy who pushes her then kisses her then pushes her again. The shower gets hot at her dad's house, but the stall's accordion door doesn't close all the way, leaving an inch-wide line of light running from ceiling to floor, where cold air streams in. Her stepmother has had an Indian woman visiting, and her conditioner makes Danny's hair smoother than it's ever been. She rinses it out and puts more in and thinks how her mother is dumb for not knowing about nice things. Last week, the two girls found Danny again in the locker room after gym when everybody had left, and the soft blonde one with the real breasts beneath her big white T-shirt told her that she should start wearing deodorant.

In the morning and before and after gym, she said.

Yeah, the tall one said, pinching her lips into the corner of her mouth.

Oh, I know, Danny said. I do.

Right, well, any kind is okay, the blonde one said. Baby powder scent is good.

The tall one looks like a dumb Olive Oyl, Danny decides. She is stupid, and Danny's mother is stupid too. Danny can't stop running her fingers through her hair, her hands are someone else's hands, and outside the door, the floorboards shift. Danny turns, and there is a blinking eye in the slit of light. Her stepbrother's chopped-up laugh rips out of him.

Get out, get out, Danny says.

She holds the accordion door to the frame with her hands.

Dad, she says. *Dad*. But he is all the way downstairs. She calls for her older sister, her stepbrother pulling against the door, squealing.

Stop it, she cries. She hears a thumping run.

Cut it out, you little shit, her older sister says. The tension on the door disappears, and Danny peeks out into the bathroom, where her sister has her stepbrother pinned against the wall.

Go, go, go, she says.

Danny grabs her towel off the hook, wraps it around her, and rushes out through the bathroom to the loft bed, where she's stacked her clothes. Her sister has her stepbrother with his arms behind him, his back and torso jerking against her.

You guys are little bitches, he says. Danny picks up her fold of clothes and hugs it to her chest and starts to run back into the bathroom. Her stepbrother wrests free and clamors to her, tugging on the back of her towel.

Stop it, she says. She screams and starts laughing, laughter like being tickled, like someone jamming their fingers into her armpits, about to make her pee, and her stepbrother tugs, and behind him, Danny's sister tugs back on his T-shirt, stretching it into a point. Danny pushes her clothes against her chest and lets the towel drop, lunging forward and shutting herself up inside the bathroom.

I saw you, her stepbrother says.

Piece of shit, Danny's sister says on the other side of the door. Get out of here. The floorboards creak, and Danny hears the empty drumming of steps on the stairs.

Are you okay in there? her sister asks. He's gone, she says.

The floor is wet. Danny's body is wet. She puts her clothes on.

My private area itches, she whispers.

THE LIVING ROOM is warm and wet, the air dense with mist. Through it all, Danny can see her younger sister curled up in the corner asleep, a Red Vine glistening between her lips, while on the couch beneath a pile of blankets, two shapes squirm and turn, grumbling and grunting like an old man, hungry. Once, in the yard at her mother's, Danny and her sisters watched a mole move beneath the earth, the ground rising along its path. They had not known what was pushing around down there, and it made Danny sick. When the mole emerged at the edge of the sidewalk, its long, oblong nose twitching and sniffing the air, its fleshy, humanlike hands grappling greedily, she contracted, felt as though a smaller Danny were falling inside herself. She couldn't tell if it was worse to know what the hidden thing was or not.

Dad.

The blanket shapes shift and freeze.

Dad?

Scram, kiddo, his gangster voice says.

Dad, I was in the shower and—

I hope you used soap this time, he says, and he and Danny's stepmother laugh.

No, I was going to say that—

You drive a hard bargain, he says, and from beneath the blanket, a handful of bills float to the floor. Danny crumples the money into a wad and shoves it into the back of her jeans.

Go buy yourself something nice, the voice says, and a string of smoke snakes up from beneath the wool.

· · ·

MARGARET HAS DECIDED THAT she is just going to tell Danny what the older boy who's maybe a man said to her. *He told me that I'm the most beautiful girl he's ever seen. And I even showed him a picture of Elle. He said she has nothing on me. He told me that I'm special and that he wants to be with me and that maybe the reason you don't write me letters is because you're jealous but it's totally normal to feel jealous when you don't have a boyfriend and your best friend does. But don't worry Tommy said that he would drive me down after school next Friday to see you for the weekend and that he would help you find a boyfriend too! It is so awesome. Don't tell your mom it's a secret, we'll call you from a rest stop when we're an hour away Tommy says.*

From the desk in her bedroom, Danny takes out a sheet of loose-leaf and a pencil. *Dearest Margaret,* she begins.

> *Thank you so much for your letters. I'm sorry it's taken me so long to respond to your many, many letters. I've been very busy with new friends who always want to hang out. Congratulations on your wonderful new boyfriend. He sounds amazing and actually reminds me of your dad. I'm sure Tommy sees all the same wonderful qualities in you that your*

dad did. I can't wait to hear all about it during your visit!

> *Your best friend,*
> *Danny*

SATURDAY DANNY DREAMS she is flying over her town. She floats above the tree line with God's view of people walking to the grocery store and driving cars and chucking bread chunks to ducks by the river. Her hair is long and golden, rippling behind her. As she flies, her body inflates, growing large; she floats higher and higher, until she reaches the sun and it whites out her vision. She wakes feeling warm and full of breath.

Downstairs, her mother is doing the dishes and sighing.

I just got off the phone with Margaret's mom, she says, turning. Have you heard from her lately? Her mother says she didn't come home after school yesterday.

No.

She told her mom that you and I were going to come get her to stay with us for the weekend.

I don't know anything about that.

She didn't mention something in one of her letters?

Maybe she ran away. She doesn't have any friends. She's not popular at all.

Oh, dear, what an awkward girl. Danny's mother

sighs and sighs and shakes her head. It's terrible not to be popular. Now collect your things to go to your father's, she says.

As Danny walks back upstairs, she hears her mother say, I am oh so lonely when you girls aren't here.

AT HER FATHER'S HOUSE, Danny takes the wad of his money and runs across the street. She buys red sugar ropes and crunchy corn shards and double-glucose snack cakes. When she gets back, she dumps the bag of food behind the bar and calls out dinner. She watches her stepbrothers and sisters wake and crawl and scramble over and divvy it all up, popping open the plastic packages and scooping candies into their mouths. In the living room, the couch is empty. On the television, a man and woman are exploring a dark cave, the man holding a lit torch aloft behind them. The woman wants to turn back. There are bugs with many legs crawling everywhere, sneaking up under her pant leg, disappearing behind her neck into her long hair, but the man insists her forward, spreading the cobwebs open before them.

Danny creaks upstairs. In her stepbrother's room, she takes the waste basin in the corner and, getting down on her knees, pushes it into the crawl space, leaving a crack in the door behind her. She takes out Margaret's letters from the back of her pants and drops them into the bin. She unscrews the silver cap and nozzle from her father's cologne and pours the pink-red liquid over the paper. She takes out a bottle of her mother's perfume called Fallen Fruit and dumps it in. She takes out a bottle of her older sister's perfume called Plum Pickens and dumps it in. She takes out a bottle of her own perfume called Whoopsie Daisy and dumps it in. She strikes a match, the sulfur pinching her nose hair as she drops the lit stick in, and a flame jumps out of the bin, enveloping her face, heating her eyebrows and hairline. Danny falls into the door, clicking it shut behind her, and kicks the bin away. The fire pours onto the floor and crawls up the wall. Danny turns and tries to open the door, pinching at the flat screws on the blank side of the handle. She kicks and punches the door. She kicks then turns to push herself against it, drawing her knees to her head and putting her head down and making herself small. The fire blackens the wall of women, their tan legs and flat stomachs and round tits, their eyes and ears and mouths and private areas. They wave in the heat then curl up blank and disappear. When the flames finally whisper into Danny's hair, licking her ears and tickling her neck, she knows she's been given a great gift, one that most girls wait their entire lives for.

INTERMISSION

I.

HERE'S THE OLD STORY: A man goes out for a pack of cigarettes and doesn't return. He begins inside a home, announces his purpose to a woman, rises, and then leaves. Never to be heard from again. A to B, here to there, easy as pie. This was before everyone stopped smoking and started running. Before phones were four-hundred-dollar rectangles in people's pockets.

We know it's not the cigarettes (though the man is a

smoker, though he's most certainly addicted), but a summer claustrophobia at his neck. Theirs is a short, carpeted nothing of a house with curling kitchen tile and all manner of moldy life in the bathroom. The living room and the bedroom are as hot and cluttered as an attic, as used up as an old hotel. The smoke of their endless cigarettes (both his and hers), bits of themselves they've discarded into the world, has soaked into the walls, become a stale reminder of a recent past.

No, not so much the cigarettes, but the woman on the couch, as there needs to be someone to leave, someone to (later) relate the leaving to others. The man closes the door behind him, and she stays on that beige and brown flower-print couch drinking whiskey or eating butter pecan ice cream from the carton, watching late-night TV, and waiting, if not for those cigarettes herself, then at least for the man's return.

There are any number of explanations for why he leaves, besides or in addition to those cigarettes. They are not the reason, but the prop, the key that turns the car on, gets the engine running.

The woman is pregnant. He gets into his car.

He never loved her. He gets into his car.

The woman cheated on him. Once, a long time ago. He gets into his car.

They don't even fight anymore. He gets into his car.

She no longer sparks him, irks him, turns him on, makes him ache. He gets into his car.

See you soon, she says with a smile.

From the couch, he standing before her, she wraps her blue-jeaned legs around his or unzips his zipper, looking up at him and then down, bemused, reaching in, digging, as though drawing a name from a hat. *Who's our lucky winner tonight?* Half-aroused, he gets into his car.

He gets into his car just as he did the week before and the week before that, occupying those tired movements as an extra might pantomime a gesture in the unfocused background of a movie scene. The car he gets into is a faded olive-green Pontiac Bonneville or Chevy Impala, a two-door car, heavy doors, low-slung and hardtopped. Any car that will take him from his neighborhood and into the world, from one life to another, because though the young man knows nothing about what going out for cigarettes means, he knows that he is not long for this life. What he would call his habits. The young man knows he needs another smoke just as sure as he needs to get into his car, addiction as inevitability, as following along with the story. It's a voice that says, Again, again. A voice that says, And now.

In every version of the story, he gets the cigarettes. We see him, from a distance, from the country road outside the lonely convenience store. He is inside beneath the fluorescent lights, taking part in that (to us) silent exchange with the male clerk. There is the turning away from the counter, the walking out of the door and back toward his car. The night air thick with cicada song, we imagine how it feels to him, throbbing hot like an open wound. And then—

Whether or not he means to leave her, whether or not the car actually breaks down.

In the simplest version, he just keeps driving. His car joins the highway in the opposite direction of his house, the taillights growing distant, their red snubbing out like the spent cigarette he tosses from his window.

In a different version, the car dies. Windows down, the man's hair loose and dancing and then the wheel going heavy in his hands. A moment, less than a second, of Aw, shit, Oh, no, Come on, not now, and then something like relief, like giving up.

Some kind of strange magic or any song that sounds like another song in that last snap of radio fuzz before it too blinks off. It's 1976. The cars are longer; the jeans fit better. The country is celebrating, but our guy thinks only of slumping deep into that uncomfortable couch in his home and feels no part of this party, feels like he's outside of time. And isn't that what getting in the car is all about in the first place? Stepping outside of some present? Moving into a different one? He feels himself cracking open, shedding some old skin. His brown hair hangs greasy to his shoulders and his mustache needs trimming, but these are only details—nothing of him cannot be changed. The car and himself in it are set on a sweeping arc to the gravelly shoulder of the road, and he relinquishes himself to its pull, the car rolling slower and slower, he feeling, knowing, that when the car stops completely, he will entirely enter his fate. A disappearance, but at the same time, a kind of birth. What better—to become part of something grander? The night is open, black and blank, and he (the car completely dead now) grabs his cigarettes, gets ready to take his first steps into it.

II.

SOMETIMES SHE GOES ALONE. As much as she likes sitting next to someone during and dissecting the whole thing afterward, she hates being whispered to, can't listen, doesn't want to miss anything. She would say that *she* knows when a piece of dialogue can go unheard or, better, when there is no dialogue and she can lean over and whisper hotly into her friend's ear or run to the bathroom, get another diet cola, and hurry back. When alone, she slinks down and puts her feet up on the chair-back in front of her, slipping on the glasses she's supposed to wear for driving but doesn't. She wishes they still played those old cartoons, the ones with the dancing bag of popcorn and soda, a vision of oversized candy boxes inside an illuminated glass case like a display for rare books or dinosaur bones. She always buys something, thinking that her extra three dollars will save the little theater. Sometimes it's a box of Dots that she'll dig out of her teeth the rest of the night, her molars throbbing; other times it's a waxy bag of popcorn in place of dinner. If she's not alone, she'll suggest to whatever date she's dragged along with her that he get something too. What do you mean you don't like popcorn? What about Good & Plenty?

Tonight the man next to her, with only the gentlest nudging, bought a box of Milk Duds. With her eyes on the screen, she puts out her palm, and he shakes a few into it. But this man is not her lover. JD is a married friend from work who also visits the little theater with a frequency he might call often, though he is not the kind of man who tries to convince anyone of anything about communal movie watching or historical landmarks. He is the kind of man whose wife knows just where he is tonight. She tells him as he's leaving the house, Have a good time. See you later. Tell Cheryl I said hello. JD's the only one Cheryl will really talk to at the printing press where they work—or rather roll her eyes to, flash a friendly middle finger to—the pair of them speaking the same quiet, sarcastic language, their jokes swift, easy things. The other day in the break room Cheryl sighed, flipped shut a magazine, and, looking over to him, said, 'The whole world is crazy except for you and me. And I'm beginning to worry about you. She sometimes worries that he'll get a better job and leave her there alone and stop going to movies with her.

On the screen before her, the man, after leaving the convenience store, after his car has broken down, walks along the shoulder of the midnight highway. There is only the darkness of his body against the blue dark of the night and the sound of his feet crunching over gravel. Then a car, low and long like his, slows down and stops ahead of him. The camera shows the man, from a quiet distance, approaching then leaning down into the passenger window. He opens the door and gets in, the car heading west, though east, the viewers know, is where the man's home lies. The camera retreats as the car moves forward, its red taillights growing dim, the scene fading to black. A beat, a breath for the viewers to wonder if this (after over an hour of film) is it, but the dull blackness of the screen then blooms into the reflective impenetrability of a pair of aviator sunglasses. The camera pulls back to include the rest of the man's face—the ruddy brown of his mustache and jawline stubble, a cigarette raised to his lips—giving nothing but the bright image of the man, the close sound of his dry breath. A further withdrawal reveals his head of hair paling to a West Coast blond and the man's open denim shirt, the wooden handrail he leans against, the boardwalk he stands on. Girls in knee socks skate past, while an old man on the ground whispers a song from behind a six-string.

Then the man is smoking another cigarette at a table outside a bar, palm trees waving before a blue, cloudless sky. A medium shot: the same denim shirt as before, but his sunglasses off his face, and a waitress, looking up, switching out the ashtray on the man's table, predicting the season's one night of rain. She leaves, and he picks up a manila envelope on the table and slides out an eight-by-ten glossy, gently gripping the photograph by its thin white border. It is an image of the man, cut off at the collarbone. His light brown hair is soft and clean, a gentle wave down to his shoulders; his mustache is trimmed, pushing out just past the corners of his lips. His mouth unsmiling, his eyes dead on into the camera but seeming to look past it, behind the camera, to Cheryl and JD and all the other viewers in the little theater.

In a soft-focused past, a woman inside a different bar sits down beside the man. She wears her long, straight hair split down the middle, and her blue-jeaned hips fill the curve of the chair's seat. A circle of beer bottles on the table, a few gentle flips of that silky blonde, backlit hair, and she's telling him he should get headshots. That he has a face both familiar and mysterious. The kind of face that makes it unclear whether he is a good guy or a bad guy. He could be anyone, she says. The man leans away, slings his arm on the back of his chair, amused by this stranger, this woman, talking to him about his appearance. Would I shave, he asks, smirking. Never, she says. Not in a million years. Everybody leaves a day or two of hair on their faces these days. She has been an extra in a number of films, she says, and once her name appeared in a set of credits as "Pretty Girl #2." As she speaks, the man shakes his head at the film titles, not recognizing any of them. He pulls out a cigarette and tosses his pack onto the table. The camera directs its attention to the woman's easy-smiling mouth. Her teeth are white and straight; soft stars of light glint from her red lips. She does not know about the wife whom the man has left at home, and she doesn't need to know. It's not about who the man was or even who he is but who he can become. Everyone here looking forward to some unknown, glossy future, as slick and beautiful as the woman's hair, the curtain of it folding around her as she reaches forward to take a cigarette from his pack and places it in the break of her smile.

The film returns to the man sitting alone in the warmth of the outdoor patio, flies buzzing around a sticky sheen on his table. Both his gaze toward the beach and the camera's proximity point to where he's dreaming: What fictitious name will accompany his own in that roll of white words on a black background? What song will play as his name slides to the top of the screen then disappears? Placing his photograph back into the envelope, he stabs out his cigarette and drains the last of his pint. He stands, replacing his sunglasses on his face, and pivots away from the camera, walking toward the sound of gulls and surf. A medium to long shot: as he walks, slowly growing smaller, the last of the day's sun fills the frame around his body, whiting him out like the flash of light people are supposed to see before they die.

The screen blackens. Off, as though someone hit a switch.

The bald, cheery owner jogs down the aisle to the lip of the shallow faux stage, the lights turning from dark to dim.

We thought this would be a good time to call a break, he says. But before we do, I'd like to make an announcement.

Cheryl, even as she has enjoyed the movie so far, admits that it's a gutsy move on his part to call an intermission. It has been a quiet, moody film without any Hollywood placeholders to explain itself to viewers. No bomb to dismantle or brass-filled, climaxing music; no hapless single woman in her thirties eating too much ice cream or tripping down a set of stairs. She has no idea what might push the film to three whole hours and wonders how many of the few moviegoers will leave.

The owner claps his hands, rubbing them together,

and makes the same announcement he's made every night for the past two weeks: In order to meet the demands of changing technology, the theater must purchase a new digital projector. Movie distributors are transitioning away from film, and the new projector is costly. Quite costly, he says. But we need it to stay open. And we can't do it alone. We need your help. He lists different donation levels, counting them off on his fingers. He has the harried yet optimistic eyes of the overworked, the underpaid, the hopelessly dedicated. See the thirty-five-millimeter films while you can, folks, he says, then runs back up the aisle to man the concession stand.

Sal. Sal is his name, Cheryl thinks, a fact she likes knowing. She's already given the recommended sixty-dollar "friend of the theater" donation, and she'll probably put a couple of bucks in the box on her way out. She'll just keep giving and giving, she thinks.

She leans back, stretches her arms out to either side, and with a soft fist, gently knocks JD in the jaw: Pow, she says. I don't like that guy.

What? Oh, yeah, funny, he sniffs. He takes out his phone, its screen lighting his face.

Last week at the bar, a man whom Cheryl had once gone out with started giving her trouble, calling her names in a voice that was too loud, that would have embarrassed her were she the kind to get embarrassed.

When JD returned from the bathroom to find the man leaning over her, both hands on the table, spitting bile, JD, in a swift, clean motion, approached, pulled him back with one hand, and, with the other, punched him in the face.

The look that flashed across Cheryl's face just then, with the man deflating into a pile on the floor—a new look surging up from some hidden wonder in her stomach: Whoa, what the fuck, JD? Not anger, but a true marveling confusion, a please-fill-in-this-blank *what*?

I don't like that guy, he responded, pointing down, one sort of fierceness draining from him, another rising in his throat.

I guess not.

Then the owner coming up, putting a hand on JD's shoulder because they were friends, because JD used to date his younger sister, Angela, in high school, the owner the real reason why they came to this bar in the first place, with its washed-out, graying beer posters and fake wood paneling, the owner, Jerry, saying, You two should probably leave.

Shit, Jerry, I'm sorry.

Cheryl up now, the three of them looking down at the black-haired man on the floor like a glass of beer one of them had spilled and then the spill sitting up, jerking away as JD and Jerry bent down to help him. JD setting him in a chair and Jerry turning behind him, asking the bartender could he put some ice in a towel, then turning back, saying, I'll give you a call tomorrow. And Cheryl, already having gathered her purse and tucking it beneath her arm like a stolen loaf of bread, led the way, she and JD slinking out, the eyes of the other patrons still on them, the place pulsing with excitement: Something happened! Just now! We saw it!

Outside in the parking lot—the night cooler and quieter—the two of them stood, not quite knowing how to stand.

Jesus, JD. You got some pent-up testosterone or what?

He walked a few strides to his left then returned. His shoulders, the broad shoulders of a swimmer, were pushed back, his arms out, tense like another man's appendages attached to his body, but then, with an exhale, his torso folded inward, chin dropping to his chest. Cheryl leaned on one leg, trying to decide what to do with her arms.

I've never punched anyone before, JD said.

Could've fooled me.

I've broken *up* plenty of fights.

Cheryl nodded to his pacing.

But I've never liked that guy. He's a jerk, he said.

No friend of mine.

Think he lost any teeth?

I don't think you got him *that* good.

He paused in his turning, spread out his hand, examined the back of it, a hand more bony, more delicate than anything else. Looking up, he asked, Are you okay?

I'm fine.

He started walking again.

Are *you* okay, JD?

Stopping, turning back to her, his legs slow, his head filled with air. Yeah, fine, he said.

She regarded the sheen of sweat on his forehead, thought of the way his anger had broken away from him. She thought of the only time she'd ever seen her mother drunk. A careful, staid woman with long, thick hair the color of dead grass whom Cheryl had only known to drink at weddings. It was the night her older sister had earned her law degree and Cheryl had met her and their parents downtown: one of the city's oldest restaurants, a small Belgian pub with black and white tile and old, round-bellied waiters. Her mother had ordered a glass of raspberry lambic and had quickly become giggly and rosy-cheeked, leaning over to ask the table next to them what they were eating that looked so good, then clapping when their food arrived. Cheryl had been happy that her mother was having a good time, that everyone had had a reason to get dressed up, get into the city, and spend some money. But she remembered feeling a twinge of embarrassment at seeing her mother's shyness and melancholy fall away, acting so unlike herself, as though people should only ever be exactly who they were.

Well, I should probably take off, Cheryl said. That's enough excitement for one night.

Right, yeah, JD said, putting his hands into his pockets. I'm sorry.

It's fine. What are you apologizing for? It was *kind of awesome*.

He sniffed. Yeah, right. Jesus.

See you on Monday, she said. And re*lax*. She was not standing close enough to put her hand on his shoulder and wasn't used to touching him anyway, so she turned, and he watched her walk away, watched her put her hand up to wave behind her.

When JD told his wife the story the next morning at breakfast, the drunk man had grabbed Cheryl by the wrist, and his face had been just inches away from hers. He hadn't meant to lie, but in the telling, JD realized that the scene was, perhaps, different than it had all seemed at the time.

But did you have to hit him? his wife had asked, scraping butter onto a piece of toast.

I know.

What if he sues us?

That guy's not smart enough to sue anyone.

Let's hope not.

Jerry said he just got a black eye.

She crunched into her toast, her face caffeinated and awake. Still, I kind of wish I could have seen that, she said.

I *did* get him pretty good.

That guy's such a bum. I can't believe Cheryl went out with him in the first place.

Well, JD started, but he couldn't quite figure out what point he was working toward. It was a small town, but even so. His wife was right. That guy was a bum and Cheryl had agreed to go somewhere with him, chat him up, and who knows what else. But even now in the half dark of the theater he doesn't want to take it back. It had felt good, natural. Something he didn't have to think about before doing, something he didn't have to mull over. It had felt like the final step in a dance he has known all his life: one, two, three—POP. JD doesn't dance but sometimes imagines swaying with Cheryl to something old and full of heartache, something by Patsy Cline or any other Technicolor singer lost to tragedy. It's not because he thinks of touching her—he keeps those kinds of thoughts inside the quiet, locked rooms of his mind— but because sometimes she seems sad and he wants to step inside that sadness with her, swim in that dark, warm pool where her laughs come out heavy and sigh-like, where she must think she remains unseen.

Are those new jeans? Cheryl asks, slumping down in her seat, her hands folded over her stomach.

Yep.

Nice.

I'm not sure I like them.

Yeah, me neither.

Then what'd you say that for?

I don't know, new clothes are funny.

She's smiling, amusing herself, but he nods, thoughtful. She sits up, digs in her jacket pocket, and offers up her flask. He sneaks a peek behind them. The other patrons are ambling up the aisle into the yellow lights of the lobby.

Come *on*, Grandma.

He bristles, taking the flask. Unscrewing its tiny silver top, he dulls his eyes at her.

You're a bitch sometimes, you know that?

I do. I'm just surprised it took you this long to figure out.

He takes as much of the liquor into his mouth as he can and swallows.

Jesus, what'd you put in here?

Peach schnapps, she says, grinning proudly.

What are you, in high school?

I was feeling nostalgic. She shrugs and takes a pull then slips the flask back inside her jacket. I've gotta pee, she says. She slides down the row away from him. Although she has the shrunken hourglass body built for tight shirts and bell-bottoms and he is tall and lean, people sometimes ask them if they're related. They usually shake their heads and laugh, but sometimes she takes JD's hand and strokes his forearm, saying, Yes, yes we are. He turns behind him and watches her disappear into the lobby.

JD thinks of how the man in the film does not remind him of himself, nor the woman his wife, even as the driving put him in the world of long childhood car rides with his parents and younger brother to Yellowstone or the Badlands. All the games they played to keep themselves occupied. I spy and license plate or Etch A Sketch, Wooly Willy—that peach cartoon face with the magnetic dust and wand. JD would put all the black dust on one side of the face, so that half was dirty with hair and the other was clean and smooth. He'd try to keep those minute particles in place as long as he could before his brother would elbow him or the car would hit a bump and mess it all up.

On the screen is a frozen cartoon of some kind of animal JD can't determine. A maniacally smiling mouse-like face with a thin snout and black, shiny nose. It's popping out of a dark circle, leaning on its rim with one arm, seeming to emerge from the screen itself. Above the cartoon's head in an old-timey script it reads, *See you again soon!* They usually put him up after the movie is over and all the credits are done. The thing is winking

and giving JD an exaggerated thumbs-up. *Maybe everything is fine!* it shouts. *Maybe you can do whatever you
want!* He thinks of the man in the car, how he left his
home for no discernible reason, moved from one place
to another as swift and silent as a ghost. Some people
can do that, he thinks, just leave. How easy it is to do
anything at all if none of it need be explained, no cell
phone ringing in the man's pocket, no letter left behind.
JD is logical, practical. He's old enough to know that
about himself, but he can't help feeling that, like the man
in the movie, his story is happening somewhere else without him. People are returning to the theater, squeaking
down in the old, springy seats, cracking their necks, pre-
paring for another hour and a half of something they
don't understand. JD turns behind him, sees a few strag-
glers in the lobby.

Outside the theater, a gentle wind pushes around a
few leaves on the sidewalk, swirls them, and lets them
fall. It isn't yet autumn, but Cheryl is anxious for it,
wants to speed it along by walking in any direction, as
though the season were a location she could travel to. A
group of couples passes in front of the theater—light
skirts and khaki pants—pointing at each other anima-
tedly, debating something hilarious. No *way. So* not true!
one of them asserts. Not just one pair, but a whole slew,
a loose mass of well-groomed citizens. Surely there is a

name for such a group, she thinks, just as there can be a pride of lions, a murder of crows. Those laughing teams of husbands and wives: A prance of pairs, maybe. A coup of couples? She doesn't know how people live inside their happiness so effortlessly. She seems to drag hers around like an unwitting child forever tugging backward on her hand. What are you doing back there? Keep *up*! When she finally gets her happiness beside her, she never knows exactly what to do with it. She'll ignore it, shout it away, or stand it up, make it do a little dance for her friends. Show all the nice people the cute thing you did for Mommy! Do it just like I showed you! Inevitably it will fail her, tripping on its black shoes or raising its white, fluffy skirt above its head. She doesn't care, Cheryl tells herself. She left it inside the theater. By now it's probably crawling around on the soda-sticky floor, tying JD's shoelaces together or telling strangers her secrets— Mommy has a *flask* in her jacket pocket, I *saw* it!

That is, of course, the way JD must see her, she thinks. A silly, brassy thing doing leg kicks and getting him into trouble. He called her a bitch. Isn't that the way she always plays it? The tough guy? She'd probably shake and shake with nervous cold were he to ever touch her. It would have to be an accident, like him hitting that man, something he would feel embarrassed about later.

A young, skinny thing jogs down the sidewalk

toward her, dark-rimmed glasses and a pair of beat-up tennis shoes. He gives her a smiling nod and a *hey* before ducking through the theater's double doors. She had allowed herself the pleasure of disappearing into the film, of watching the man move through its world with no purpose, like watching a pair of neighbors through a window silently eating dinner. It was more than just how it looked—the past of the film giving it all a matte, grainy mystery, a this-kind-of-thing-doesn't-happen-anymore glow—but there was something disquieting in its moody anticipation, a feeling that the more that nothing happened, the worse it would be when something finally did. Or nothing will happen, Cheryl thinks. The film will just keep going and going until it stops—no climax, no big coming-to-a-head scene, no resolution to take home with her.

She wishes she smoked. She never knows what to do with her hands when she's outside doing nothing. To that group of couples, she must have looked like she was waiting for someone. Shoving her hands in her pockets, she walks toward the dark, wooded park across from the theater. When she gets to the end of the street, she crosses and keeps going. She thinks about going home, what awaits her there. She will pull her dark hairs out of her hairbrush, twist them into a coarse ball, and throw them away. She will call in sick on Monday and maybe

the day after that. Or she won't call at all, won't tell anyone. Let them imagine, for a time, their lives without
her. Taking a left down an unlit street, a canopy of dark
trees that will soon lose their leaves, she sees JD sitting
in the theater, adjusting his cap, sighing, as the movie
begins again. With films like that one—quiet, difficult
to understand, meaning kept hidden—she won't be
surprised when the little theater doesn't make it.

III.

OR, BEFORE GOING OUT, he receives a letter. We see him
returning from work, retrieving an envelope from the
small, rust-colored box just outside his front door. The
envelope is plain and white but asserts its presence for
not being a bill—no tiny cellophane window to peek
through—and for the name on the front: the man's own.
There is a return address from a Spanish-sounding name
of a town in California. It is the only mail this day—the
envelope thick and soft, many pages—and he takes it in
the house with him, opening it alongside a bottle of beer
at his small kitchen table.

The sheets of paper within have been folded into
thirds. *Dear James*, the first page begins. A thick black
ink, a decent pen. Looking back to the return address,
the man wonders who knows him in California, anywhere near California. The letter instructs James to

copy—either by typewriter or by hand—the letter and its accompanying pages, a text written by the letter's previous recipients, and then to add his own paragraph at the end. He's to do this three times and send each letter to a different person within three days. The letter's author—in a boxy, forward-leaning handwriting, neither masculine nor feminine, neither script nor print—goes on to detail the fates of previous recipients who did not follow the instructions. A woman in Ohio was strangled by her husband of fifteen years, he having accused her of cheating. A boy, a teenager, took his dog for a walk in the forest preserve a mile from his house; the collie returned two days later without him. Car wrecks on long stretches of night highway without another vehicle for miles; allergic reactions; sudden, previously unknown medical maladies; amnesia. The man has never been a member of a team, has always been wary of groupthink and anything that involves a number of people doing the same thing at the same time: school choir, church, disco. More something his superstitious wife would be into. He flips to the next page. Above a solid block of text, in the same pen as the first page, hangs the title: An Old Story. In some versions, he keeps reading.

In the movie version, the wife is a crone, a controlling, uncaring woman whom we want to not only see left but also shamed, made to realize the ways she's failed. If only she had been kinder, the man's car wouldn't have broken down. The wife's hair is stringy and limp, her eyes the insensate gray of the drugged. She barely lifts her gaze from the boxy television as the man leaves the house, goes back to watching a made-for-TV movie, a woman with long, glossy hair found dead, bent and angular, in an alley. It makes it easier, in this same version, for the man sitting in the theater—after having sat for too long, after having given the woman too much time to walk away from the small, old theater—to finally rise, rush up the dark aisle through the lobby's soft, buttery light, and out into the now-damp chill of evening. Easier for him to look one way down the lamplit street—always the wrong way first—then the other. To run now, to turn the corner, to see her from afar and call her name.

In most versions, there is no man. No unreliable car or woman with hair like silk, hair like curled ribbon, hair like old string. There is no short house to leave from, no dimpled couch sunken into a shrug or pieces of chicken in a cardboard bucket next to a six-pack of Schlitz in the fridge. In no version is the night warm, romantic, or mysterious. No version in which the season means anything at all. After a few years screening adult films and B movies, the single-screen theater in the small town closes and does not reopen for many years, if it ever reopens. Instead of a house, there is a blank, dry field near the interstate. There is the distant whoosh of passing traffic that sounds like fabric being ripped. Bottles and old pieces of pipe in the dead grass, crumpled paper garbage that has been tossed from above, and at the front of the lot, an orange plastic fence that arcs downward in a lazy collapse. In one version, there is a FOR SALE sign pushed into the earth and people who might do something with the space. In another version, there is no field.

HERE COMES
YOUR MAN

THE MAN DRIVES A TRUCK and has a glorious beard.
It's leather brown and looks impenetrable, like the
after of a Just for Men commercial. He says, You probably wouldn't be interested in someone like me. We're in a
bar on the edge of a college town, and my friends and I
look like the grad students we are. They don't understand why I like to come here, where there will be people
we don't know.

What department are you in?

History, I say.

I would have guessed science.

Because of the glasses?

They're dark-rimmed and thick—massive. Some-one once told me I looked like Woody Allen in them. Not the exact compliment a woman wants to hear, but I don't mind. It's kind of true.

What kind of truck do you drive? My dad used to work for Peterbilt.

Oh yeah? It's a—

How much room is there in the cab?

IT'S COZY IN THAT little bed area behind the seats. The cushion takes up the whole space except for small cub-bies in the walls. One has a tiny TV/DVD player in it; another is tall and holds a rack lined with Carhartts. The trucker places our shoes in an empty recess, tucking in the laces. He's taped up a bunch of old-fashioned post-cards on the walls. Lots of pronouncements from states that don't get enough attention. *Iowa: You Make Me Smile. Missouri: Let us show you the Show Me State!* I like when young people collect old things. A way to say: everything used to be just a little better before. It makes the trucker seem interested in his world but not overly clever, like he's not going to be making any jokes I don't get.

I came straight up from Missouri, he says. Didn't even stop at home. I just needed to be around *people*. He looks at me and smiles, scratching carefully beneath the rim of his dark knit cap. I've suddenly grown shy, always more interested in good lines than in actually delivering on them. It's crowded with the two of us back there, and when he finally puts his arm around me and we take off our clothes, it is as though our lovemaking is all a complicated way of saving space. *You know, we'd have more room if I could just put this* here *and you put that* there ... It feels like Tetris, like packing boxes in a different kind of truck, and I think maybe I *should* have gone into the sciences. All that spatial reasoning, something about conservation of energy.

Afterward, we lie perfectly creased into each other's bodies.

I say, You must be really good at folding maps.

He says, You're beautiful.

I bite my lip.

I could get used to this, he says, and I wonder what I've gotten myself into.

HE JUMPS OUT of the truck then helps me down, and I have a vision of women wearing laced-up boots and full, complicated skirts, of a man pulling them from horse-drawn carriages. What kind of hat would I wear?

He wants my number. He lives here and wants to see me when he's in town.

How often are you here?

A couple days every couple weeks.

It seems like the right amount. He hands me two scraps of paper—one with his number on it, the other blank. I've left my purse inside the bar. The trucker looks like a bigger version of a dirty, whiny folk singer I like. His cap is now off, his hair an unkempt overgrowth on his head and face, his lumberjack jacket zipped all the way up. I want to tell him who he reminds me of, but instead I write down my number, because he only *looks* like a singer-songwriter. I trust he will not whisper in infinite harmony with himself about his ex-girlfriend. He'll just be.

As he pulls away, he looks down at me from his perch. I crank my fist up and down, and he pulls his horn. Haa-honnn.

Inside the bar my friends have quarantined themselves at a corner table, debating the Teapot Dome Scandal. They wave their arms and throw their heads around—a flock of pigeons pecking at the same piece of garbage. When I say hello, they look at me like they forgot I came with them. The virgin I've been seeing narrows his eyes at me and asks, Where were *you*?

THE NEXT MORNING I call my grandmother. It's my grandparents' sixty-eighth wedding anniversary, and I tell her congratulations, my voice sounding small like a child's, something that happens when I talk to her. I ask her if she and Grandpa did anything special today, and she laughs and says with a sigh, Ohhh, no, nothing special, just the usual. They went to church, she says, and ate lunch at the local family restaurant. It's called Family Restaurant. I can immediately recall the limp pickle spears and sheets of iceberg that came with my burgers from Family Restaurant when I was a kid, how my dad would pull fries off my plate and replace them with sprigs of parsley. How he would order a tomato juice and shake pepper and Tabasco and A.1. into it, then below the table tip vodka in from a pocket flask. We'd cheers as though drinking champagne, tiny bubbles popping in my soda. I tell Grandma that sometimes the old places are the best ones, and she agrees and asks me if it's snowing where I am, only a couple of hours south of where she is. There's snow on the ground, I say, but just a little. Then we talk about how much we like snow—this is the Midwest and we like snow—and she says that she and my grandfather shovel the walks themselves, but that the high school kids still cut through the yard and muck it all up. I tell her that the mailman does the same thing. Although what I say is true, I'm partly talking for effect—I hope that she will appreciate me, someone much younger than herself, complaining about disrespectful people ruining my perfect blanket of snow. I tell her how

I wait for the mail, getting really excited, and how nothing good ever comes. Bills, offers for credit cards, coupons to fast-food restaurants. On Sunday evenings I watch *60 Minutes* just for Andy Rooney. I want to trim back his eyebrows the same way I want to clear the ice from the walks. Grandma says, Your father used to *love* to shovel the walks when he was a kid. He'd do the whole block without even being asked. She's been doing this to me a lot since July. Laying out some little piece of something that I never knew about him and can no longer ask him about. I'm glad she tells me this stuff, but all the details—snow shoveling, his Cub Scout badges, serious, unsmiling yearbook photos—seem misplaced and wrong, like excerpts from another man's history.

I'VE ONLY BEEN OUT with the virgin three times, but he already wants to DTR—define the relationship. This, apparently, is a thing. He's chosen the only hip restaurant in town—the dark place with red, glowing lights and little white plates—to do this. I look around at all the other tables where people wear dark, slim-fitting clothing. Surely they know what's going on. They see his white-blond hair, khaki pants, and small, contained face, and they know.

The thing is, though, I kind of want him. I want to take him out and mess him up a little. I just can't help it.

Our waitress comes. She looks like a model, as skinny as a Pall Mall. I don't smoke, but will sometimes crave a cigarette harder than anything. I'll bum one, take a few good drags, then remember why I don't smoke. It's not about the filling up of my lungs, but the gesture, making those movements with my hands, letting people know that I'm too cool to care about what happens to my body.

So how many little plates should we order? I smile up at the waitress. I want to somehow signal to her that the virgin and I aren't really together, that I'd much rather buy her a fancy drink and kiss her cool, thin lips, or at least hang out, brush her long, silky hair, and talk about boys.

As many as you'd like, she says.

I look at the virgin. He's got his nose in the menu.

I circle a block of tapas with my forefinger and she leaves, taking the menus with her. The virgin finally looks up and gives me a tender smile, but then lets it drop. It's serious time.

So, he says.

So, I say.

So I was thinking about going down to Springfield this weekend.

Uh huh.

They've got the new Lincoln library. Have you ever been? I've heard it's amazing.

The virgin is a Lincoln Studies Scholar. This designation exists in only one program in America, our very own university. I picture a Lincoln beard over his face, something he could put on and take off like those Groucho Marx glasses, but the image just gets me thinking of my Russian ex-boyfriend who had the most excellent thick black beard. He was always screaming at his mother over the phone in Russian: "*Nyet, nyet, nyet!*" I loved it when he fought with her; I loved it when he told her no. When he'd hang up the phone, I would pull him down on the bed and fuck him, thinking of how much his mother would have hated me had we ever met.

So what do you think? he says. I mean, well, what do you think about us? He looks as earnest as a *Sesame Street* character.

Well. I clear my throat. You're a fine person to sit next to in a movie theater—you let me eat nearly all of the popcorn, and I never worry about you talking to me during. I trust you as a driver, even if you're a little on the slow side. You always signal well in advance, which I appreciate.

Cassie.

You have really nice breath. Not to be underestimated. It seems like you eat an Altoid maybe fifteen minutes before we see each other—it's not too strong, but it's clearly there, definitely lingering.

Cassie.

The waitress brings a round of little plates. She barely fits them all on the table, their lips overlapping.

Well, this all looks really good! I beam. Each dish is delicately arranged, the foods glistening in their oils. I roll my silverware out of the napkin. I don't know where to begin.

Cassie?

We eat quietly. I take exactly half of everything. When the food is gone, I excuse myself, go up to the bar, and ask the bartender for a smoke. I give him a one-sided smile, like I'm not trying too hard. I take it outside in the gray, slushy snow and choke the whole thing down in front of the restaurant's big glass windows, so that the people both inside and outside can see me.

THE TRUCKER'S NAME is Roger. When he calls, I ask him how old he is, because the only person I've ever known named Roger was my father's best friend. My father's Roger was a carpenter, skinny as a rail, and had a har-har-har style of laughing. I think of how My Father's Roger sounds like a pretty good name for an alt-country band.

I'm thirty-two, he says.

Oh.

How old are *you*?

Twenty-four.

Ah.

So doesn't your name get a little funny over the CB radio?

Yeah, people have some fun with it.

Yeah, like in *Airplane!*

What's that?

You've never seen *Airplane!*? I think of how my dad used to say, And don't call me Shirley, at least once a day, it seemed.

Sometimes they just call me Rog.

Rog, really?

Yeah.

Huh.

THE VIRGIN AND I drive down to Springfield. I've decided to see where this might go. He's seemingly forgotten about the other night, now too geeked over all things Lincoln to worry about relationship definitions.

It's twice the size of any other presidential library, he says.

Twice the size, huh?

And this is the only house that Lincoln ever owned.

Lincoln's bedroom is on the second floor of the house. There's a dark wooden rocking chair and matching four-poster bed. A tiny bedside table. We stand just out-side the room with the other visitors behind a looped rope. Mary had a separate room, the tour guide tells us before leading the group downstairs to the sitting room. The virgin moves to follow, but I tug his hand.

Hey, I say.

He smiles.

I let go of him and step over the rope.

Cassie! he whispers.

Tiptoeing across the room, I wave my hands just above the surface of a dresser, as though an invisible force field protected it. I open an imaginary drawer, take out a hat, place it on my head, and admire myself in the mirror on the wall. I walk back to the doorway.

Don't you want to get a little closer?

Well, he sighs. He's not even looking at me.

Lincoln *slept* in this room.

He's leaning in at his waist, peeking around the cor-ner, getting in as far as he can without actually entering.

The lady said the carpets aren't original. It doesn't matter if you get them dirty.

Whoa-kay, he breathes. He steps over the rope as carefully as if the Great Emancipator were still there sleeping. With the pace and reverence of the grieving, he silently walks the room, finally stopping next to me beside the bed.

Is it everything you imagined? I ask.

It looks a little different up close, he says.

I take his hand and gingerly guide it over the white quilt. He sucks in his breath like he's been shot.

I turn and sit down.

Cassie.

You can't tell me you haven't thought of this. He finally laughs, his face loosening, his eyes traveling to a place just beyond us—beyond this room and house, beyond school and work, beyond the Land of Lincoln and into the Land of Yes.

Mr. President! I exclaim and pull him down on top of me. I bury my head in his neck and put my arms around his skinny waist, but he wriggles, slides off me, falls to the carpet, then gets up quickly.

Jesus Christ, Cassie!

He's out, stepping over the rope, creaking on the floor to join the rest of the history buffs downstairs. I fall back and let my head drop to the bed, wondering whether Lincoln traveled to Mary's room at night or she came to his.

I GO TO THE MUSEUM. Sit on a bench in the great hall next to the life-sized replicas of the Lincoln family. Abe, Mary, the kids. I'm feeling a little Mary Todd–ish. A little buttoned-up and restricted, as though, like that famous first lady, I too have a head injury beneath my bonnet. In college, I dated a Lincoln reenactor. Now, I'm not a tall person. Only a little over five feet. We got some jokes, no doubt, but you couldn't blame them. That boy was a lot of limb. I think of the trucker and traversing the trunk of his body like a hardened landscape, like tundra. I spot the virgin at the other end of the museum. He's walking down one of the branching hallways, getting smaller and smaller. The Lincoln reenactor had an amazing beard. It was dark and real. It had to be; they were serious about that shit. He played the Civil War Lincoln, memorized the Gettysburg Address, but even so, I would sneak up behind him when I caught him sitting, would push my finger to the back of his head.

The virgin comes back into the great hall and catches me staring at Lincoln's crotch.

Let's go, he sighs. He's done with me. I'm over. And now he knows it too.

On the ride home, he does a good job of not talking to me, even when I turn up the radio so loud it hurts my ears. He lets me out, and I tell him to hang loose. His mouth moves, but I can't hear anything he says because the Pixies are growling about ceasing to exist, about giving one's goodbyes. He's looking straight ahead, shrugging, moving his small, tight lips. I imagine him saying that I'm silly, loose, depraved, but the thought stays with me as long as Frank Black's voice does after I close the door. I put up my hand and wave.

I mean, you can't help but wonder. He *was* the tallest president.

IT DUMPS A FOOT of snow on us, resetting the landscape to something cleaner. The trucker texts me to say that he won't be able to make it back to town until next week, but that he wants to have dinner when he returns.

I stay inside eating toast and drinking milky tea. I'm reading about the Bay of Pigs, but I keep taking breaks to masturbate. This has been going on all day, and by now I've lost count. My head feels like it's bobbing a few rooms away from the rest of me. The rest of me moves slowly, and like a cat, I follow the sunlight coming through my windows, lying down in each bright, heated square. Once I'm warm, I get back into bed. I worry about how some smells never seem to leave the things that hold them. I'll have to scrub and scrub. I think about first going to the virgin and giving him my hand. *Here's what's missing*, I want to say.

THE NEXT DAY I run out of jam. Wild grape and elderberry. My grandma makes it from scratch. It's the only kind I'll eat now. It's dark and earthy, the deep purple of a gemstone.

From the porch, I see her inside shuffling to the

door. I sometimes fear that they won't hear the doorbell and I'll forever be left standing there, waiting to be let in.

Hello, sugar!

I bend down to hug her. She's as soft and lumpy as a pillow and smells like old wool.

Herb! she calls behind her. Herb, Cassie's here! She pauses to listen for him, then looks back to me and shakes her head. We sit down in the living room—the couch, chair, and rug are all the same shade of country blue.

Did you have trouble driving with the snow?

No, they've plowed all the roads pretty well by now.

Well, you be careful out there. Don't drive too fast. Her eyes are light blue and clear as glass. I've been thinking, she says, if we make it to our seventieth anniversary, you'll have to have a party for us.

You'll make it to seventy, Grandma. But I say it with as much certainty as anything. I don't tell her how now I can't stop imagining getting hit by a bus or falling down a set of stairs. How I sometimes try to decrease my chance of certain accidents by staying inside all day.

Well, we'll just have some fun while we can, hm, sweetie? She turns to look behind the couch into the kitchen. That man, she sighs. Let's go down there and bug him.

The walls leading to the basement are covered with pictures from old *Life* and *MAD* magazines my dad put up as a kid. The Beatles and Mia Farrow. Doris Day with a mustache drawn above her lips. We walk down into the cool air, and it's like stepping into a pool: one moment outside and the next within. The same old smell of damp and dust.

Oh! Oh! Grandpa says when he spots me, doing a little jog over, opening his skinny arms out wide. He hugs me tightly, and it feels the way it always does, bony and a little painful, but mostly good. He gives me a shake and then releases me.

You came to get some jam, did you?

I nod dutifully.

It's been a *while* since we've had any elderberry, he says. But let's see if we can't dig some up.

I follow them through a door and then another one. Shelves are laid out on either side of me, stacked with scrap wood for burning or building, used cans of spray paint. My grandparents disappear into a dark side room, and I stop to dig through a red milk crate of vinyl records. A feeling of cool fear comes over me flipping through the albums, not finding anything I recognize. I have no idea who could have owned anything by the Carpenters.

We've found something here, Cassie!

My grandma is just on the other side of the wall, working her way toward the doorway between us. Your father used to love this! she says, but I'm already backing away. She says something about how quickly the weekend goes by, and behind her, Grandpa replies, All the snow will melt soon enough, Fran. But I can't listen. It is as though their voices are arriving to me from a future that does not include them. I turn to go upstairs. It's cold down there, and I've forgotten why I came.

THE TRUCKER PICKS ME UP in a small maroon car. It reminds me of boys I knew in high school.

Where's the truck?

He laughs. You think I drive that around town?

Oh, right.

I turn behind me. I think about climbing in the back later, but it doesn't have the same allure, none of the tight order of the truck cab. There's something embarrassing about his tiny car, his tininess within it. And he looks different, his hair no longer hidden beneath his cap, something open and bare about his face.

Where to? he asks.

I suggest the hip, dark place with the white plates. It's a joke, but he takes me seriously. I want to say that he wouldn't like it there, that the lighting, the music, everything about it is delicate and precise—pretentious—but we go anyway.

At the table, he squints into the menu. So a bunch of little things, not a regular entrée. He purses his lips. I can tell I'm going to leave completely sated, he says, nodding.

A different model-waitress from last time takes our order and comes back with red wine. We touch glasses ceremoniously, and when I bring mine to my lips, some dribbles down my chin. This always happens. It's like I'm throwing it at my face and just hoping some makes it in.

I have a drinking problem, I say. He laughs, though I know he doesn't get the *Airplane!* reference. I realize now what it is about his face. He's trimmed his beard. What was once thick as Bluto is now like lace, snow-white pieces of skin visible across his cheeks.

So your dad used to work for Peterbilt?

Yup.

Retired?

He's dead, actually.

Oh, I'm so sorry.

That's all right, I say. He doesn't mind.

He pinches his brow.

I mean, what are you gonna do?

He tilts his head, a tentative smile shaping his lips. He clears his throat.

So what kind of truck did he drive? Local? Long haul?

Long haul, I say, and he nods slowly, as though he just correctly guessed my zodiac. I don't want to explain that my dad never drove the trucks. He only worked on the engines, taught people how to fix them, but that it kept him away nonetheless. He only wore plaid on the weekends.

You know, this place isn't *horrible*, he says, looking up at the Edison bulbs hanging from the ceiling.

No, not horrible, I say, grabbing my glass, not spilling any this time.

AFTER DINNER I convince him to take me to the truck yard. I jump up and down and tug on his arm until he says yes. There is a long line of semis, staggered as neatly as a card trick. I can't tell which one is his until we're beside it and I'm climbing up the little ladder. We get in the back, and I start jumping on him. I bury my head into his armpit and try to push him over. I crouch up and fall down on his chest, he taking my weight like he's wrestling a toddler.

Jesus, girl, settle down! he says, laughing. I'm really spazzing out; I can feel it. But I can't stop myself. My laughter comes up like seltzer.

You're out of control, girly!

I told you I had a drinking problem!

Shirley, you must be joking.

Hey, I thought you said you'd never seen that.

I watched it the other night.

I've got him in a bear hug. I want to turn him over. I'm grunting and straining against his bulk, but he doesn't move.

Hey, come on, settle down. Let's have a conversation.

Bor-ing. I climb over onto his back and whisper in his ear, You're a lumberjack and you're okay. You sleep all night and you work all day.

His body finally comes alive, and he yanks me around to face him, grabbing my shoulders. Let's get out of here, he says.

I crinkle my nose: I want to stay. I try to shrug him loose, but his hands hold my arms down. I drop my head to my shoulder, my neck feeling vaguely whiplashed.

What's going on with you?

I shrug my shoulders. He's trying to look into my eyes, which only makes me sad. I cross my arms and shrink a little. I want to move and keep on moving, but I've lost my verve.

Let's just drive somewhere. Do you have to make a run?

A run? No, he sighs, shaking his head. He dips his chin to hide his smile. He's patronizing me now, I can feel it, but I don't know how to explain to him that I don't want to know anything outside of his cab, where everything is small, where everything has its place. I think of the virgin. How nice it must be to know all there is to know about a dead president but nothing about what he did in his bedroom. It feels right, as close as we should get to any one thing. The trucker drops his hands from my shoulders. His body is as thick as a buoy; if tossed into the ocean he would float forever. His hand is warm when it touches mine, and at first I want to pull away, but I take it and squeeze. I squeeze as hard as I can, like I'm gripping a pair of those springy hand grippers, like I'm trying to break them. I look at him. He looks back and squeezes my hand just as hard. His face has become serious and rigid, his warm eyes sunk to somewhere darker. It starts to hurt. I want to ball up my other hand and punch him in the face; I want to bite his lips. I want *him* to bite *me*. But we stay right there, him squeezing my fingers hard enough that I stop feeling them, his hands and arms so big that he could fold me up and shove me into one of the storage compartments, stuff me inside the little closet. I think of how cramped it would be in there with all his jackets and work boots and movies, how, with my arms pushed to my chest and the door shut, I might never get out.

GIVE AND GO

THE PROBLEM WAS THAT THE MAN was too tall. Or the woman too short. He didn't want to lord over her. She didn't want to be so far away from his mouth. She wasn't the kind of woman to wait, to pine, to wish and hope and pray to someday maybe be kissed. If she wanted to kiss, she was probably kissing. The man knew this about his friend, appreciated that directness, and so on their walks, and on this walk in particular, a basketball tucked beneath his arm, her striped athletic socks pulled up to her knees, he found himself slouching, while she pulled herself up as tight and tall as ever, her large breasts pushed out forward, as though guns ready to be fired. What more could she do? Ask him to stop so she could get some height from a concrete planter? Hook her foot in a fence? He, sensing her frustration, sometimes wondered if it wouldn't be best to just get it over with and pick her up. She was heavier than most short women he knew—the elastic of her sports bra pushing out the excess flesh of her body—but he was stronger than he looked and wouldn't mind the strain. He thought this consciously, held it out before him in his mind, that this kissing, this coupling, was something he should do, but he couldn't bring himself to close that last bit of gap between them. He'd broken up with his girlfriend of two and a half years at the beginning of the summer, and he saw how something had turned on in the short woman. He felt a sudden desire, could sense her pushing, pushing, nearly running in his direction, this forward momentum forcing him to unfold a thought that had lain closed in him for some time—that he might not like women or men for any kissing whatsoever. The feeling left him slack and weighted, filled with sad guilt that he couldn't return his friend's big desire. Like today, all their walks took place in the middle of the afternoon, the summer heat drawing sweat from their necks, no time at all, the tall man reasoned, for two people to smash their faces together anyway.

When they made the turn toward the outdoor court, the pair saw them warming up. The group was running drills and shooting layups, doing a little give and go. This was the man's favorite part: walking slower, hanging back to see his friends exposed as they were in their mesh basketball shorts and shoes, their nasty old T-shirts with the sleeves cut off. In five years, they would be too old. One had already gotten his ankle good and twisted a few months ago, and nobody could make it the full hour anymore without having to sub out. But there they were, clumsy and groping, calling out to each other in the waning hours of the summer afternoon, tossing up bricks, letting their voices get nice and loud.

After stretching, they divided themselves into threes, the tall man and the short woman on the same team. She gave hard, ugly passes to the man, who converted them into layups, at turns graceful, at others scrappy and ragged. If he missed, he'd scramble and elbow to his own rebound and go up again. Those not guarding him held back on the perimeter, slowly retreating, watching him push the ball up and over the lip of the rim with an ease they no longer knew.

The woman was guarding the dirty-blond wisecracker on the other team. He was scrawny, but beneath his faded gray T-shirt was the promise of a drinking man's belly, pale skin, and a swirl of dark, wiry hair. She pushed her torso into his and threw her arms into the open spaces his limbs made.

Hey, hey, he said, you're going to have to buy me dinner first.

It wasn't the only time he'd made this joke with her. He stepped back, smiling, and still dribbling, said, Lil G, I can't help but notice how you *always* seem to guard me.

They called her Lil G. Even the tall man found himself saying it, though no one had ever before called her the name. The others encouraged her, overencouraged her, it sometimes seemed, though only in hindsight did the man wonder, Too much? He did not want her to think their encouragement was false, which would be worse, he decided, than no encouragement at all. Whereas she, in the moment of play, always thought, Oh, God, please stop, wondering why every unmade shot was met with clapping, with, That's okay, Lil G, keep taking those. Keep trying.

Body-checking the wisecracker, she lunged for and got her hands on the ball, dribbling up to half court.

All right, all right, that's a foul, little lady.

I'm sorry?

You fouled me.

She stopped dribbling and tucked the ball into her hip. I did not foul you. If you want me to foul you, I can show you what that looks like.

Whoa-ho, he said, putting up his hands. If you want to get close, all you have to do is ask.

Give me a break.

Come on, Lil G, everybody saw it.

She looked past him to the others. Any of *you* see anything?

Well . . . the big guy in the headband said, looking down.

She raised her eyebrows at the tall man.

It looked like a foul, he shrugged, but I couldn't see that well.

Fine, whatever. She shoved the ball into the wise-cracker's stomach. I'm just going to get it back anyway.

He bent down low and started dribbling, and she crouched down there with him. He passed the ball off to the big guy in the headband, who backed himself toward the hoop. His soft backside bounced off the tall man's bony pelvis, once, twice, three times. The tall man had the feeling, because of the physical similarities and differences between them, that this pushing back and forth, one against the other, could go on indefinitely, that neither of them would ever grind the other down. He could smell the sweat of the big guy and the sweat of himself, but mostly it was cut grass and flowers hanging their heads in the heat, and some other wet scent that he could not name as either earth or flesh. The big guy, getting nowhere, tossed the ball back out to the wisecracker, but the woman jumped for it, her hand tipping the ball to half court. She and the wisecracker scrambled and fell upon the ball, the concrete of the court peeling skin from their elbows and knees. They pushed and pulled with the ball between their hands, she finally wrenching it free and, from the ground, throwing it out to no one in particular. The tall man jumped forward to receive it and, turning, seeing an opening in the lane, charged ahead past his friends, whom he loved, but who were not as fast as he was. He dug down low and, springing up into the air, stretched out his body as long as he could against that sea of pale, loose arms. There was a strain and pulse in him, his arms circling and jerking, which made it seem like he wanted to go in several directions at once but couldn't decide which. He took the ball in both hands, drifted up to the basket, and, pushing the ball through the hoop, hung on to the rim for what seemed like a very long time.

He came down hard, so hard that pins and tingles jetted up from his feet through his legs, and the muscles in his jaw and ears clenched tight. And yet he felt joy, such big joy in him, as a single, beautiful line pointing in any one confident direction, that he wanted to cry out in gratitude for being given what he'd been given, for doing what he'd done, which he knew, despite the adrenaline and life coursing through his body, would never be repeated.

Fuck yeah, he breathed. Fuck. He watched the ball roll off into the grass behind the hoop, where it came to a slow but certain stop. He turned in order to find the others, to open his body up to them, but his friends, their arms and mouths slack, were facing half court. There the woman and the wisecracker were still down on the ground, fighting over something. The tall man took a step forward.

Straining against each other's skin, their sweaty arms grappling, torsos squirming, the two of them wrestled each other's sticky shirts over their heads, before shoving their faces together.

Holy crap, headband said.

It's about time, said the bald one.

The tall man stood behind the rest of them. The pins and tingles returned, moving around with so much ecstasy in his limbs that he couldn't make them do what he wanted them to, which was get him so much closer. He wanted to get as close as he could, to see if the energy there might pass into him, that they might all share it, but he stayed back, watching his friends watch their friends do what they needed to do. The man on the ground scrunched his face into the woman's neck. The woman on the ground pursed her lips and exhaled, as though in pain, as though blowing out a candle. The sound the two of them were making reached their friends' ears before the breeze disappeared it in the brown leaves swirling in the open court, while the sun, noiselessly tucking itself into the horizon, put a sharp golden light on all their beautiful bodies.

NEEDLESS TO SAY

'M IN THE SHOWER TRYING to shape a piece of my
hair on the wall into an M. My hair's long, but it won't
hold the letter's turns. It looks more like a snake essing
toward the end of the stall, where it might eventually
flatline or curl into something unrecognizable. I used to
do this with Emily when we were younger. I'd put my
hair on the tile when she was going in after me, and later
she would come into my room with a towel around her
head and say, I love Eric Barnes too, or, You're not fat,
picking up the conversation as though I'd spoken aloud.

We'd sit on my bed, pulling threads from the seams of my quilt, and I'd tell her what I wasn't able to before. But those talks only lasted a few seasons at best, and there have been so many seasons since then.

SORRY, EM, I'm trying to spell out, because I know she's feeling down, but it looks more like SORRIES, and I think about just scrapping the whole thing. I want my meaning to be clear.

Part of the problem is that this is my sister's house. She wants me to act a certain way in it. Wash the dishes after I've cooked, keep my feet off the coffee table. Emily is younger than I am, but at some point she seemed to pass me by. Getting degrees, getting married. Our older sister, Joan, is more or less out of the picture, and I guess Emily felt like she had to fill the gap with regards to leadership and adult progress. But it doesn't bother me. I kind of like being taken care of.

The other part is that Emily's husband, Will, used to live in this house. That is, until six months ago, when he caught her having an emotional affair with the manager of a La Quinta a few towns over. She's the manager of a La Quinta here, and the two of them met at some regional what-have-you conference. At least that's what our cousin Stacy told me. Stacy is no stranger to gossip, so if she knows something, then it's safe to say that everyone else knows it or will know it very soon. Needless to say, it was disappointing to hear this kind of thing secondhand.

Anyway, Will ended things and took half their stuff with him to some resort town in Arizona, a place where they probably still have a few real quintas hanging about, so now Emily needs me. That's what Stacy said. She was the one who suggested I move in, help out around the house. Provide *moral* support. I've decided I'm more of a seen-and-not-heard moral supporter, like someone bidding on a silent auction. Emily doesn't talk about Will, and I don't like to mention sore subjects if I can avoid them.

If I had to put a name on it, I'd say Emily just seems distracted. That is, she concentrates very intensely on things that aren't Will. She moves around the house with a focus so acute as to eliminate the thought of anything but the task before her. She scrubs the kitchen backsplash until the enamel starts to wear; she eats apples like she's punishing them for ever having existed. The socks I leave on the living room floor get her very focused indeed. And she's always on the phone with work. Our parents left us a nice amount of money when they died, which made employment, how shall I say, *optional*. So it still surprises me when she leaves the house in the afternoons wearing a blazer and chunky black shoes, or when I hear her talking about a "perfect sell," which I first heard as perfect *cell*—C-E-L-L—as though all the hotel rooms were cells, like in a prison. How odd, I thought. Those manager types sure are cold! But a perfect sell—S-E-L-L—is when all the rooms (or cells) are full. That's her goal every night, filling the rooms up with people.

Ours is a shitty college town, and I can't imagine anyone coming in on a Tuesday to check out the pool hall on Main or the bowling alley across from the twenty-four-hour laundromat, let alone enough people to fill an eighty-four-room La Quinta every night. But somehow she does it. She cares very intensely about certain things, which also seems to be part of the problem. She cares so much, and it sets her up for some real disappointment. I, on the other hand, take pleasure in life's smallest details. For example, I'm really proud of some other things I accomplished in the bathroom this morning. So proud that I was thinking of leaving some evidence behind for Emily, but her sense of humor has been off as of late, and I'm trying to be sensitive.

After showering, I go for a walk. It's only eleven, but already the heat is serious, so I stay in the shade and move as slowly as I can without stalling out. I like to make my time outside the house last.

I turn onto the street behind the grade school and a squirrel bursts out from a pile of cut grass. Mother-fucker, I hiss, my body tensing with reflex. The squirrel immediately scurries off like it just grabbed my wallet. Come back, little squirrely, I say, but the damn thing

has already disappeared. This town is filled with squirrels. They were imported some hundred years ago from
England, and now the town is overrun. I can't drive to
get a gallon of milk without hitting one, almost hitting
one, or seeing the poor, bloody result of someone else
having hit one. Their bodies lie out flat in the road, their
gray, puffy tails quivering in the breeze like a flag casting
a warning.

The library's automatic doors open before me like
welcoming arms. I love it here—the return slot with its
tiny rubber conveyer belt, the weekend book sale, the
take-no-prisoners air-conditioning. And the librarians,
whose sole civic duty seems to be to act nice to me. They
know my name and ask me how my day is going, what is
new in my life. I tell them, Oh, fine, Oh, nothing. And
then I do my loop around the whole place. New music,
new movies. I go upstairs to the magazine racks, ascending the wide blond steps. The light comes in through the
floor-to-ceiling windows, and I step into it, enjoying the
feeling of being in a place of beauty and importance. I
check all the new issue covers—glistening pictures of
cakes and shiny, famous faces and cartoons of animals
in business suits. The weeklies, the monthlies, it all helps
me mark the time. Like going to work, like it's all something the town needs me to keep an eye on.

Sometimes I'll chat up the young man at circulation.

The library has automatic checkout stations, but I figure he must get bored just standing behind the desk waiting for someone's card to mess up. That and I like looking at his face. Everything about him is angular yet soft—his linen shirt is tucked into his khaki pants and his brown hair falls over his eyes. Refined, but not too refined, like someone who attended prep school on scholarship. I'd put him around my age, but sometimes he scolds me for keeping a particular book or movie too long, and it makes him seem older. I like it when he *tsk-tsks* me.

Hey, Claire, he says.

Hi, Thomas.

He shifts my stack of books across the counter and gets to rubbing them over the magnetic plate.

How are you all doing? I ask. Super busy?

Well, the summers always are, but we handle it all right. He smiles and then shifts his gaze to his computer screen.

I'm not really doing too much these days, I continue. Well, my sister—I'm taking care of my sister.

Oh, dear, is she all right? The concern in his voice takes me aback.

Oh, yeah, she's okay. Just a little psychic malady. Nothing a little sun and St.-John's-wort won't fix. It keeps me busy, but I have some free time too.

I then hint to him how good I am at organizing *other* people's stuff and how it might be fun to work at the li-

brary myself, since I'm here so often, and, no, I don't actually have a library degree, but I *do* own a couple of
different pairs of glasses, several pairs of dark-colored
tights, and slip-on shoes that don't make a whole lot of
noise when I walk in them. So, you know.

You're too funny, Claire, he says, shaking his head.
He slides the stack of books back to me over the counter.
Which do you think you'll read first?

I sigh and pick up the titles one at a time.

Well, *Charlotte's Web* is always a good one. I like the
drawings. And *Mrs. Frisby and the Rats of NIMH* is
pretty cool. I like imagining their little outfits. And *Old
Yeller* always brings the house down . . .

I'm noticing a theme here, he says.

What? Animals? I look down at the names.

Yes, and, well . . . Maybe you'd like some of the
books *upstairs* too.

Upstairs?

You know, Virginia Woolf. Oscar Wilde. I bet you'd
like Dorothy Parker.

I purse my lips. I've heard some of those names, of
course. I went to college—for a couple of years—but
they don't feel like anything I need.

Maybe when I'm finished here, I say, and I square
my stack and give it a pat.

. . .

EMILY, LET'S GO to Sal's.

Emily turns a page of her book.

Emily, Sal's, I repeat.

Today is her day off, and we've had a very civilized, quiet morning of reading and drinking iced coffee in the living room. I'm so restless I want to peel my skin off and wear it as a housecoat.

Emily, Sal's.

That place is gross, she replies.

Come on, you need some more stuff around here.

I think I can do better than the Salvation Army. She doesn't look up from her book.

Not better deals. *Not* better deals.

I can afford new things, she says.

But you might find a real find there. *Find a find.*

Find a find? I feel like I need a shower after coming back from that place.

Then we could go swimming at your work. After.

Gross.

Please, please, Em. (I'm good at begging, I know. It's a talent and I like doing it.) Come on, why not?

I don't feel like it, so why should I?

You know who you sound like, don't you?

Finally she looks up from her book. She gives me her sweet death eyes—angry but also amused by my brashness, like, *Ooh, someone wants to get hurt, do they?*

Fine, she says, her smile slow and controlled. I'll get my purse. You drive.

I KIND OF LIKE to say *estranged*. We're estranged. Our estranged older sister. The word feels luxurious, filled with mystery, as though we have a crazy woman up in the attic giggling maniacally and setting fires, a woman trying desperately to kill us. What I wouldn't give to have spent time in an orphanage!

The problem with Joan was there was never a standard deviation; there was no room for error. You either gave her exactly what she wanted or it was *No, no, no. You're doing it wrong.* We don't like to admit the ways we're becoming like her. *You know who you sound like, don't you?* It's our greatest insult, but we use it sparingly to maintain its pungency. We discovered rather early on that *bitch* meant less and less the more you said it.

Three years ago. The morning after Christmas. The four of us crammed around Will and Em's apartment kitchen table. Red and green and blue lights framed the archway into the living room. We'd just finished our coffee and pecan pie breakfast when Joan carefully pushed her plate aside, cleared her throat, and said, *So.* (She had such a way with beginnings!)

So. She said it was nearing the one-year anniversary

of our parents' death, and she wanted us to mark the time by putting their remains into the wind. We need to *scatter* them, she said, like it was a word we didn't know. She lived two whole time zones away, a coastal extreme, but thought we should meet where our parents had lived the last year of their lives, which would mean a plane ride into the desert for Em and me. The plane our parents had been in returned to the earth soon after leaving it. But the distance was enough. Having us get into any flying machine seemed like Asking For It. We could drive, but Emily would have to reschedule her dress fitting and work wedding shower. She turned to Will for backup, but he'd slid into the living room to play his new single-shooter video game, a pair of headphones over his ears.

Can't we do it another time? I asked. Does it have to be the exact anniversary? I didn't say so, but I also had plans. A group of kids from downtown had recently taken a shine to me, and they were gearing up for a rager of a Groundhog Day party. I didn't want to miss it. I liked how they had no jobs and never talked about their pasts or asked too many personal questions.

It doesn't mean we don't love them, Emily said, her voice quiet and explanatory. But surely we can wait. I've got so much going on before March.

Joan took a long breath in and out, putting a hand to her forehead. I just know if we don't do it now, we're never going to do it, she said. It threw me how strong her feelings could be—her voice a heated whisper—when they were so different from my own.

Months later, at Em's wedding reception in Gold Room B of the downtown La Quinta, Joan told us she'd done it herself.

I'm sorry that you were too busy having a shower, she nodded to Emily, and partying with children, she wiggled her fingers at me, but I couldn't wait.

You had no right to do that, Emily said.

I *had* to.

We asked you to wait.

I told you we couldn't. They're our parents.

I wanted to say, *Were, were* our parents, but I was trying to resist any feelings that might put me in the coatroom for the rest of the night.

And where are you partying? Emily turned to me.

And who uses "party" as a verb anymore? I asked.

They both gave me a look that said, *Now is not the time to get smart.*

Luckily, Will bounded up just then, his suit jacket missing and his tie threatening escape. Sorry, ladies, he said, but I've got to take my *lady*. Before I could tell him that he needed to work on his delivery, he whisked Emily away to cut the cake into its separate pieces.

One week, two weeks, two months later, Joan didn't call us, so we didn't call her. Or, we didn't call her, so she didn't call us. I know it's silly for it to still matter, but it's hard to break the status quo, no matter the status, and I'm not really the leader of this outfit. It all leaves me with that morning-after-Christmas feeling—seeing our unwrapped presents stacked individually in Em's old living room, the tree heavy with inherited ornaments. That's the thing about Christmas. I love the trees and the lights and the garland, but I want to take it all down as soon as it's over.

I ALWAYS FEEL a little odd driving us anywhere. Like I'm underage or drunk or otherwise unfit.

Emily's got her phone to her ear, listening to a voicemail, and I can hear a deep voice unfolding from the tiny speaker. She closes her phone and puts it in her bag.

Was that La Quinta? I ask.

I've taken to calling her mystery dude "La Quinta," which brings to mind a man with a thin, dark mustache and bolero jacket. I imagine him saying Emily like *Em-ee-lee*, each syllable a sexy little secret between the two of them. In reality, he probably has adult acne and wears a lot of polos.

We're not talking anymore, she says, and looks out the window.

Who was it then?

My doctor's office.

What do they want?

For me to call them.

What for?

I don't know. She digs around in her purse and then pulls out a tube of chapstick.

Aren't you going to call them?

Later.

You can call them now. I don't mind.

That's okay. She rubs the balm over her lips then replaces the cap as on a stick of glue.

I park in the back at the Salvation Army. We open up the double doors. The warehouse is scattered with piles and piles of stuff. Clothes, housewares, books. No shelving, no clothes racks, just pile after pile, like an industrial yard full of garbage waiting for a band of hoboes to come along and set it all on fire.

This is the wrong one, Emily says.

No it's not, I reply.

She drops her shoulders. You've got to be kidding me.

There are two Salvation Armies in town. The regular one, the one with eighties blazers and bins full of balled-up scarves, and the reject one, the one that takes all the stuff that doesn't sell at the regular Sal's. We're at the reject one, the one that sells by the pound.

I approach a pile. Shoes without their mates, bras the color of stained teeth. I pick up a vase.

Look at this *vase*! I hold it up like a trophy. It's purple with two turquoise dolphins on either side. They're curved into S's with their heads pointed up, mouths open in smiles.

That's nice, Emily says.

Don't you love it? I can't believe it didn't sell at the other place.

It's truly a wonder, she says.

I wonder how much it costs. I weigh it in my hand.

You're not buying that.

I want it.

You're not bringing that thing into my home.

But look at them—they're making a heart with their bodies. Their *dolphin bodies*. They're saying, *I love you, other dolphin!*

I don't care what they're saying.

They're mammals, I reply, as though their possible relation to eels were causing the holdup.

She stuffs her hands into her shorts and walks down the way, too quickly to really look at anything.

I get back to the pile. I tuck the vase beneath my armpit so I can pick up an old rubber doormat, but when I stand to examine it, the vase takes a dive to the floor, and one of the dolphins cracks off. At the far wall, an employee heaves a bag of garbage over his shoulder and walks toward the exit. I push the vase pieces back into the pile with my foot, hoping they'll be able to keep themselves together in all that mess.

I SKIPPED A COUPLE OF DAYS of washing my hair, so when I shower this afternoon, gobs and gobs come out. I pick it from my palms and place each strand on the tile. Emily works the four-to-midnight shift, and most days I manage to get in before her. It's just that sometimes the hair dries. It curls away from the tile and falls to the tub with all the intention of leaves from trees.

IF YOU WOULD LIKE TO TALK

It seems clear, but I worry about how she might fill it in: *I have the number for a great therapist. You should try journaling. Maybe Will was just kidding!*

I LIVE DOWN THE HALL

And I can't help but wonder how long it will be true. That maybe if I don't break any of *her* vases, she'll keep me on as a partner, a sort of life assistant. Sometimes I go to the store and buy these gluten-free crackers I know she likes (though I often end up eating half of them when I'm home alone). I let the water run a half hour more and splash some onto the wall to make sure my message doesn't fall away.

A COUPLE OF DAYS LATER Emily and I are lying out on the side of the La Quinta swimming pool. Short green bushes run along the perimeter, and on the other side of them we can see the tops of semis as they drive by. It's barely eleven on a Monday and we're the only ones out here. Tiny speakers hidden in the bushes pump out crackly dance tunes—a little Motown, a little funk. A man is singing about how his woman is as sweet as or sweeter than honey.

Emily's wearing a white short-sleeve button-up and a pair of loose chambray pants. When we arrived and she didn't undress, she said that even on her day off, her employees should not see her in a bathing suit.

You're going to get an awful farmer's tan, I said.

She only shrugged and opened up a magazine.

Hey, Emily, check this out. I stand up and take a running dive into the deep end of the pool. When I come to the surface and look up, her head is still tilted down, her eyes covered by her big sunglasses.

Did I splash?

You jumped into a pool of water. Of course you splashed.

But a big one? I ask, hoisting myself up onto the side of the pool.

Yeah, a big one.

I want her to rank me—8.3, 9.2. Like I said, these small things, these *seemingly* small things, are important. I walk over to the table between our chairs and open up a bag of salt and vinegar chips. There's something satisfying about my body dripping wet and the chips be-ing dry and crisp inside their bag.

This is fun! I say, sitting down in my lounger. We never get to hang out.

We hang out all the time.

I meant before, I guess. I crunch into a chip. Aren't you having fun? I ask.

Not really, no.

Emily's phone rings on the table between us. She looks at its face then presses a button on the side, silencing it and turning it over. It could be La Quinta or the deep voice from the other day or someone else entirely. Emily rubs her eyes then moves her hand to her chest, letting it rise and fall there.

Emily, I say.

What. Her head is down, her face hard beneath her sunglasses.

The music has clicked over to a funk song with lots of bass and brass. I stand up and start doing this dance I made up where I pretend my arms don't work. I leave them dead and hanging and get them flopping around by moving my legs and torso.

Emily.

I'm not looking at you, she says.

I move so that my shadow is cast over her. I twist back and forth so hard that my arms fly up and hit their opposite shoulders.

Stop it, she says.

Em, I don't know what's happening—my arms don't work.

You look like an idiot, she says, but I know she doesn't mean it; her mouth is smiling without her permission and her shoulders start to shake. This is my favorite part. When she's laughing at me but doesn't want to. When she tries not to encourage me, but her smile keeps cracking through.

Stop it! she cries. She pushes her hand into her smile as though to crank it back down, unable to stand the way we give each other joy.

BACK AT HOME, I pass her room on the way to the shower. The door is cracked and I can hear her soft crying.

Em? I push open the door.

She's sitting on the edge of her bed. She raises her face, eyes red-rimmed and too wide, like I've caught her at something. I walk in and lower myself next to her, and the depression of the bed sinks our shoulders together. The water in my hair, full of chemicals from the pool, has bled through my T-shirt and dampened my back.

Will was never really my favorite person, I say.

She lowers her head and sniffs.

He was always a little goofy, a little cheesy for my taste.

She slowly shakes her head.

Didn't you tell me once that he got all of his jokes from a book? A joke book?

She puts her hand to her brow.

And, truly, the incessant video game playing was a little tired, like maybe he was kind of a cliché? Of a dude? Who plays video games?

It's not Will, she says, breathing deeply. She rubs at her eyes and gets to telling me some things. She goes back in time and then moves forward. I sit beside her, and it takes so long, me not saying a word, that my hair dries up into its natural curl and the light of the day passes over us.

IN THE SHOWER, I don't have much loose, so I work my fingers through my hair and tug. I tug and tug until I have enough.

I'M NOT LONELY WHEN I'M WITH YOU

It's all I want to say, but I wash and condition and pull out more in the rinse. I gather it into a loose disc the size of my palm and smush it onto the wall in case she needs it.

THOMAS THE LIBRARIAN has written down some names and numbers on a piece of paper for me. I'm searching them out with the grave intensity of an Indiana Jones type, imagining the reward to be bigger than a bunch of books. It was endearing to watch him do his job—his face wrinkling with thought, writing with one of those little golf pencils. He sends me to Fiction first, then Science/Health/Medicine and Biography, then back around to Poetry. It feels like I've been given a map to a foreign city or a set of very complicated instructions. By the time I'm done, my arms and chest ache with the books' weight.

It would be easier if it were just one book, I say, relinquishing the pile to him.

What book would that be? he asks. His smile is soft and curious. He scans the books, one at a time, dissembling my stack on one side then making a new one on the other.

How to Be, I say, shrugging. *How to Get from Here to There. How to Help Yourself . . . or Others*.

Well, here's a good place to start, he says, and slides them to me.

THE FOLLOWING WEEK I'm sitting on the edge of Emily's hospital bed, surrounded by pink balloons, pink cards, and a spray of boldly, unnaturally colored flowers in a vase. I made the mistake of talking to Cousin Stacy when she called me the other day, and now it feels like a bunch of people have come over uninvited.

I've got an idea for a movie, I tell Emily. She's tired but awake, quiet.

She sighs, less annoyed than usual, which for her is like saying, *Yes, please tell me all about it.*

Things keep going wrong, I say.

She nods her head and swallows, a movement she makes look painful. They put a tube down her throat for the anesthesia. It'll be a week or two before we know for sure how everything went.

But then maybe at the end things start to go right again, I say.

There's a quiver at the side of her mouth. That's stupid, she whispers. Her eyes are down.

Why?

Because you can't just tack a happy ending onto something like that. It's cheap. It's not real. She closes her eyes and swallows again.

I regard all the balloons and flowers on the two side tables. Pink, I think. Nobody knows us. I grab a gift mug from behind one of the vases. It's big and white with pink, looping script on it, filled with candy wrapped in gold, crinkly plastic.

Hey, look at this! I say. I can't tell in which way I'm trying to cheer her up. The ironic, *Can you believe this shit* sort of way, or the *Hey, believe this* way.

She takes it in her hand, reading the inspirational message on the side. No doubt she's wondering when these words ever worked or what simpleminded soul they might have worked on. She turns the thing over and drops the candy into her lap, rears back, and, despite the bandages, throws the mug across the room. It hits the opposite wall with a ping. I go over and pick it up. It's mostly fine, save for a spot on the rim, now chipped like a tooth.

I look up at her with golden eyes. Now we're talking!

I bring the mug back and set it on the table in case she wants to throw it again. Emily doesn't know, but I made a few phone calls earlier. One to the man she used to be married to and the other to you-know-who. Will's voicemail voice sounded needlessly chipper, like nothing even close to bad had ever happened to him before. You-know-who was a muffled ghost, her voice startlingly the same, as familiar to me as my mother's or Emily's. I don't know when they'll get back to me or what will happen when they do, but I'm trying to manage my expectations, to think about it in such a way that any outcome will be desirable. Like this vase of flowers. After the leaves fall off the stalks and the night nurse comes and throws it all away, dumping out the stinky water, I tell myself it won't be such a big deal.

THE SUMMER FATHER

THE FATHER ARRIVES every dead summer to drive the girls west. No destination named, only a direction and the promise of mesa, mountains, stone-dry heat. Two weeks—the longest uninterrupted time they spend with him all year. They pack sleeping bags and pillows, Roald Dahl books, T-shirts, and bathing suits. It is the four of them in the cab of his truck, the short trailer hitched behind. A tape deck and three tapes. The shift from mother to father is swift. *Do you have everything you need?* A hug, a hug, a hug, and a wave.

At rest stops the girls imagine a mirror family on the other side of the highway, except they envision a father and a mother, a son or daughter or both at the end of her hand or hands. The girls do not need to say or even think that a father with his daughters is not like a mother with her daughters. At the stops, losing him for minutes, they coalesce, become a team. Three girls among women washing their hands, three girls among women's bodies, the air thick and hot, the sweet smell of a stranger's shit. In the lobby they look at state maps set behind glass, the red You Are Here dot. *We've gone this far, are going to go this far.*

In the afternoon, the father gives the oldest a thin fold of bills, and the girls run into a gas station to gather Corn Nuts and Twizzlers, Milk Duds and fun-sized bags of chips. They each choose the same kind so regularly that the father made a song of it. Or the father made the song and the girls oblige it. When they return to the truck he snaps his fingers and whisper-sings, *FRI-tos / CHEE-tos / And po-TA-ta chips.* They like the way he defines them, even arbitrarily, even through slippery plastic bags of processed corn and sodium. *This is who you are, who you can continue to be.* He isn't there at home. He doesn't know how the middle daughter has been taking hour-long showers at night, how nobody knows what she does in there for all that time. How the oldest, only twelve, came home from the movies with a hickey not two weeks ago, and then sulked at a family party in the backyard, eighty degrees and she red-faced and sweating in a turtleneck. The youngest, the mother has determined, will need braces, despite having quit sucking her thumb last year. He no longer day-to-days it with them, never really did even when he was in the house, and so the jingle. My little *munch*kins, he says, getting back on the highway, as though tickled at being a father, at having these three separate pieces of him beside him reading books, housing secret desires and preferences each her own. He sets the cruise control and turns on the music, a favorite song with funky piano and brass. Hey, he says, and bobs his head until the youngest and the middle join in. It's like this, he says, gesturing with his hand, and they mimic him, as obedient as backup singers. The oldest, only twelve, nearly thirteen now, sometimes sullen, sometimes pouting, looks out the window, crosses her arms over her breasts, breasts she's been hiding under big white T-shirts, breasts whose sudden existence has the father calling the girls' underwear *unmentionables*: Don't forget your *unmentionables*. I've washed your *unmentionables*. C'mon, the middle says, pushing at the oldest's shoulder. She hates how the oldest must now be convinced to participate, hates her creeping sense of power, as though her presence were a gift and one to be doled out judiciously. They have to make her forget the girl she's becoming at school, the girl who quietly gets straight As but who hangs out with the tan, popular girls, *is* one of the tan, popular girls now, girls getting new bras, girls who let boys suck on their necks in the back row of their small town's single-screen movie theater. At home her sisters try to coax her into her previous self, an old dress that still fits but which she is sick of. What's wrong with it? her mother would say. You used to love that dress. C'mon, the middle says, and bumps her again. The middle shakes her shoulders, as if the oldest— only twelve yet moving exponentially beyond her ten-year-old sister—merely forgot how to do it. Cut it *out*, she replies, and the middle says, Fine, jeez, and keeps dancing. Her movements are more contained, now only pretending to have fun, so as to show the oldest she doesn't need her.

The middle sister was there that night at the theater. She sat up front with her best friend, who, a third of the way in, nudged her and whispered, *Look*, and the middle turned to see her sister in a far corner with some skinny, freckled boy on her neck, her face stiff, eyes open. The middle looked back to the movie, now lost as to who the characters were, why they were doing what they were doing. The middle did not tell the mother, though she wished for her sister's punishment. She watched her mother discover the thing on her neck the next morning, breathing the oldest's name like a curse, and dig out the turtleneck so that she could play ping-pong and eat potato salad and sit on the backyard swing staring into nothing.

When the song ends and the father rewinds the tape, the intro building again, the middle says, *Come* on, one last plea that's no longer pleading, a tone that says, I know what you're doing, I know why you're doing it, but isn't this more fun? The oldest angles away from the middle then looks back over her shoulder. She smirks and moves her eyebrows up and down. The middle snorts.

Stop it, she says.

What, the oldest says. I'm dancing. She shakes her shoulders slyly.

Dance normal.

I *am* dancing normal. She closes her eyes and shakes her head back and forth, hopping in her seat, her hair whipping around her face. It's a real freak-out! the oldest says. Seeing her, the father hams more. He closes his eyes and uses his fist as a microphone. The middle joins in as the brassy payoff returns, and for a moment, they all coordinate, punching their fists in time to the chorus. This will be the last summer like this. Next year, the oldest will insist on cheerleading camp and the father will instead have them for a week at his house. There will be trips to the park district pool, where the girls will eat nachos and Italian ice and look at boys and call their father to delay when he'll pick them up. The music is just louder than loud, and it opens up a good feeling inside the middle's chest. It makes her uneasy. As on the last day of school when she and her classmates had written their names and addresses on slips of paper tied to balloons and released them in the parking lot. She watched her balloon rise—one among the dozens—up to the tops of trees and beyond, a shrinking yellow dot.

THEY DRIVE THROUGH the night. The father buys coffee; the girls run into gas station bathrooms—tired yet alert and giggling—the dull yellow lights swirling with mosquitoes. The girls go into the back of the capped truck, where the dad has laid out a futon and a pile of blankets. The highway lights run one after another over the truck as though propelling it forward. The middle loves the late-night driving hours, hours usually kept away from her. Fifteen years later, after the father will complete his slow, early death, the middle sister will think of those together-yet-separate hours on the night drive: she and her sisters dozing, her father up front, a slit in the window for his cigarette smoke to slip out of. Always there will be the same wonder: What did he think in those adult hours? Who was he then?

IN THE MORNING they stop at a small-town McDonald's, eating outside in the bright, early sun. The street, lined with trim green lawns, leads to a stoplight and a row of antique shops and bars. After they eat, the father lights a cigarette and spreads out the atlas. The oldest, sitting at the next table, leans over her book.

The middle takes the youngest a block down the street to a park, clambering up the curving metal slide, running across a wobbly wooden bridge. They climb on top of the monkey bars and crawl on hands and knees. She sends the youngest back, watching her dash across the empty street, and walks over to the swing set on the other side of a tall, needle-thick pine. They learned it as an accident, at the beginning of the summer at the playground across the street from the mother's house. A swing set with a metal trapeze bar hanging from two chains. The oldest sister and her friends would, one at a time, wrap their legs around the angled support beam and slide up, so they could sit on top of the high bar and swing. After a while they stopped going for the bar, only sliding up then down the beam. It tickles, one said, and the others laughed, the middle standing, watching. Three weeks, three bored summer weeks while the babysitter and the youngest sister stayed back home under the ceiling fan, eating ice-cream sandwiches and watching music videos. Then the oldest sister and her friends stopped going to the park. There was a girl down the street with a pool and a mother who worked nights. You can't come, the oldest said, and bought a bikini with her own money.

The middle sister felt betrayed but knew she would have repeated the betrayal to her younger sister if she'd been allowed to join them. The next week, on the night of the movie, the oldest and the middle stood outside the theater waiting, and when the oldest sister's friends arrived, she joined them in a circle—arms crossed, their long, thin legs sprouting out from bright cotton shorts. A girl one grade ahead of them passed by, a girl with big brown hair and a cropped white shirt, with pink and purple beads at the ends of its tassels like a jeweled curtain. She walked with one hip out ahead of the other, and it made her look at once filled with attitude and injured. That girl is a cunt, one of them said matter-of-factly, and the others snorted. The oldest looked behind her, and the middle, leaning against the theater's brick exterior, turned her head to pretend she hadn't heard. The unknown word put a blood-taste in her mouth. Metallic like the smell of the bar she leans her body on now. She closes her eyes. Her breath is slow and quiet, the only sound she hears but the wind in the trees, the distant whisper of a car. She slides herself up the bar until the tickling feeling leaks out of her. She slides down, her feet crunching into the bed of pebbles, and her older sister is behind her saying, You shouldn't do that.

She turns. A shameful heat opens in her stomach so fast it's like she's wet her pants. The sun is bright around her sister, the upward slope of her small, tanned nose, her brown hair hanging at her shoulders, but she looks like someone different. The middle's heart beats big inside her throat.

I wasn't doing anything, she says.

Yeah, right. That's gross.

It's not gross, the middle says, but there's no conviction in her. She cannot feel good about a thing she doesn't have a name for.

It's time to go, her sister says.

Back on the highway, the middle starts crying. Silently at first, but her heavy breathing gives her away.

Are you crying? The father leans over to look at the middle. He does a triple take between her and the road. She turns away from him, and her shoulders start to shake.

No, no, no, what's wrong? No, it's okay.

What? *Really?* The oldest looks at her, leaning in. Are you kidding me? She sighs and looks out the window.

The middle hangs her head, trying to make it so that neither her father nor her sister can see her face. What's the matter, the youngest asks. The father fumbles with the tape deck.

Hey, c'mon, he says.

Everybody's attention gets her going harder and louder.

Oh, jeez, says the oldest.

I miss Mama too, the youngest says, putting a small

hand on her shoulder, and it is like when the middle is sad at home and their border collie noses her cheek. Her face crinkles, and the youngest starts up too. I wanna go home, the youngest says.

C'mon, don't you start now, the father says, hitting play on the stereo. The music comes blasting out in the middle of the song. He turns it up louder than before, and the two cry harder.

Hey, hey, the father says, motioning with his hand, a bigger version of the dance they did earlier. The youngest moves deeper into the crying until it gets away from her. The father turns off the music, and the middle stops abruptly, wiping her face with the back of her hand. She swallows and the father reaches over to mess her hair.

THE DRIVE GOES on and on. Flat, open, dull. An anxious, geared-up lull. Time crackles and breaks once they enter the park, as soon as they see the brown official sign announcing its name in white, carved-out letters. The father tells the girls to hop out. One on either side of the sign and one at the bottom. The middle and youngest put their arms around it, as though it is a fifth family member. They collect these photographs the same way people buy magnets or badges or tiny spoons with the park seal stamped on them. They don't have the money for these trinkets, and though the girls secretly, separately, desire them, they have come to view them with disdain, as a frivolity they don't want anyway.

They follow the park road up the mountain, one side in shadow, sunlight pushing through fat clouds on the other. The campground is on the north rim of the canyon—dry pines, shadow and sun, pale dirt. A handful of colorful tents dot the spare forest. The girls don't see any other children, just middle-aged couples scattered among the dozen spots—men with gray beards, women wearing bandanas over their long hair. They make a slow circle around the sites then take a spot on the edge. The father backs the trailer into the thin slice of tar pavement, then clips the pay stub onto the signpost, claiming the spot as their own. Some people have wooden plaques with their names in burned-out letters hanging from their trailers. THE JOHNSONS. THE WARNERS. These are the same people who put potted geraniums outside their trailer doors, the same who roll out a carpet of fake grass beneath their striped awnings. A home away from home. The middle sister never saw her parents kiss or hug—nothing like it—and now there are only listless waves from cars or front porches, flat-toned telephone conversations in which the mother tells the father that the girls shouldn't eat so much candy. When she is twenty-five, the middle, alone in an art museum in Toronto, an otherwise unremarkable, unmemorable museum—a large, modern thing—will walk through a curving hallway into a white, open room, completely empty but for a man and a woman on the floor kissing. Their bodies longways on the blond, lacquered wood. The man will be on top of the woman, the two of them rubbing against each other with a slow, deliberate intensity. She will think their passion is a performance, some unmarked exhibit. Even so, a heat will swell in her stomach and her face will grow red, suspended in the eroticism of no possible relief or release. Stopped, standing in place, she will resume her slow walk at the edge of the room, so as not to appear taken, affected, anything. She will keep the couple in her periphery. The woman, blonde like her, her jeans tight around her ass, the man's hands at her waist. Nothing will stop them; they will give no sign they know she is there. The middle will carry the memory of the couple for years but won't tell anyone, won't remember anything else about the museum or the pair except the careful distance she kept between herself and them.

THE FIRST STEP INSIDE the camper shows everything shifted, disrupted and wrong, as a house recently burgled. A cabinet door open, a box of cereal on the floor. They put it in order. They take the cardboard box of newspaper off the floor, place it out next to the fire pit. The middle and the youngest unroll their sleeping bags on the bunks by the door.

What are we going to do after this? the middle asks. Are we going to have a fire tonight?

Of course we will, the oldest says.

They drive to the visitors' center. They wander through an exhibit on railways, another on how glaciers formed the canyon thousands of years before. They see the area's animals, stuffed and behind glass. A chipmunk clutching a branch. A mountain lion hunched on a high slab of rock. They read about what they eat, their prey and predators, where humans might see them. They play a game matching the animal to its tracks and droppings. The plaque reads, *They're all you'll ever see of some species.*

Returning to the site, the father climbs onto the trailer's bottom bunk to take a nap. It is the hot, quiet slump in the day, and the cars and trucks are missing from the other sites. The oldest reads at the picnic table, and the middle and youngest hang together in the hammock.

When are we going home? the youngest asks.

We just got here, the oldest says, not taking her eyes off her book.

Two weeks, the middle says. Like last summer.

I want to talk to Mama.

You can't talk to Mom, the oldest says.

Why not?

The pay phone is all the way down at the entrance. It's too far.

I want to talk to her.

We can tomorrow, the middle says.

The youngest wedges herself out of the hammock. The middle watches her walk to the trailer and step up onto its metal step.

What are you doing, the oldest asks.

I want to see if Dad will take me.

He's sleeping.

I want to talk to Mama, she says more insistently.

You'll hurt Dad's feelings, the oldest says.

The youngest crosses her arms and sighs, stamping over to the fire ring and huffing down onto a fat log. Her face crumples and her chest heaves.

Hey, c'mon, the middle says. Don't cry.

You guys are such babies, the oldest says.

The youngest puts her thumb in her mouth, her brow knitted, angry and concentrating. She wraps her other arm around her stomach. She closes her eyes, and her mouth starts going, her face softening. Her mother did so much to get her to stop last year. At night, she duct-taped socks over her hands. She rubbed fishing lure gel on her thumbs, but they would find her in the morning with the socks torn off, the gel smeared around her mouth like melted ice cream. The mother kept socking her hands, and the youngest kept ripping them off. Stubborn, stubborn, then she stopped cold, and it seemed like that was that. Around this time, the youngest started bringing her toy vacuum cleaner into the bed to sleep with her. Nearly the length of her body, a white, smooth plastic, its base a clear dome inside of which whir tiny Styrofoam balls when it's pushed. She calls it by the neighbor boy's name, a boy with a head of tight blond curls whom they see out at the beach club the mother's family belongs to. Her sisters tease her whenever they see him, draw out the syllables of his name in a long *Oooo*. At night, she lays an arm and a leg around the toy, and the mother, worried about the youngest's teeth, lets her keep it in her bed, as though it were nothing more than a stuffed animal.

The youngest's cheeks hollow and fill, making small sucking noises.

Stop it, the oldest says.

The youngest's eyes stay closed.

Hey. The middle says her name.

Stop it, that's gross, the oldest says again.

Just let her, the middle says. Seconds ago she was tempted to get up and pull her sister's thumb out of her mouth herself, but she feels her allegiance turn sharply on its heel.

You used to, she says.

Yeah, well, I stopped because it's gross.

It's *not* gross, the middle says, standing up, her arms stiff at her sides.

No, it *is* gross. It's disgusting and she shouldn't do it.

You're a cunt, the middle says, her eyes quaking.

You don't even know what that word means, says the oldest.

Yeah, I do.

Oh, yeah, what?

It's someone who's *mean* and *slutty*.

Like that the oldest is up and on her, pushing her into the hammock, leaning over and punching her skinny arms. The middle puts her arms over her face and kicks out with her legs. The youngest sister stands and wails, her eyes closed, arms loose at her sides.

The middle rears back and kicks her older sister in the chest—a bony, dull thump—and she falls into the dirt. Her face is a mix of pain and anger, reared up, then—just as fast—restrained and put away. The middle stands up and moves away from her, the oldest says, I hate you, the youngest wails, and the father throws open the door of the camper, screaming, What the hell is going on goddamnit, shut up.

THEY WIND DOWN to the park entrance and find a pay phone, each of the girls taking a turn. The youngest sniffles, says she wants to go home, can't the mother come and get her, and then she goes silent, listening. She nods and nods, bucks up, and gives the phone to her sister.

The middle says, She started it, says, She's so mean, I never want to be like her, and the oldest cries, finally, silently, turning herself into the brick exterior of the liquor store. There is the liquor store, a gas station, and a closed antique shop on this stretch of road, and nothing else. A grassy field behind a barbed-wire fence and beyond that the mountains they came here to see. Be good, the mother says to each of them, not be good for your father, just, Be good. The oldest and middle are made to apologize to each other before the father takes the phone, his voice a tight whisper.

They drive to the grocery store. The father's is a summer birthday, and in the fluorescent lights of the aisles, the girls go off on their own, find a boxed cake mix and the accompanying ingredients. The oldest reads the list, leading them to the right sections. When the middle skips ahead and returns with a carton of eggs, the oldest says, Good job. They slide it all onto the back of the checkout conveyer belt, the father pretending not to see and then paying for everything. When they return to the site, he starts a fire and reads the local paper at the picnic table. Inside the trailer, the girls mix the cake's ingredients, bake it in the tiny stove, following the directions adjusted for elevation. They poke their heads out the door at him and giggle, and the middle has that feeling again. Of the joy filling up and overflowing, of wanting it and so bad but knowing it as something that will peak then float away. It makes her giggles come up fast and nervous, edging out beyond her control.

The cake turns out funny—overcooked in some spots, wet in others. Still they cover it in unctuous frosting, pour on sprinkles, and push in blue-and-white-striped candles, and when they emerge from the trailer, candles lit, the father acts surprised. He says, My little *munchkins*. There must be a moment, the middle will think later—candles lit, the evening sun cutting sharp through the trees—when he feels he is alone. The father's house is not a home. It's the place where he lives. A squat house filled with itchy furniture and cigarette smoke. The girls will not remember the cake like he will, the undeniable adult feeling of getting older. The father wrinkles his nose, says, Daddy's a geezer, and groans and goofs like an old man.

After cake, he says, Spread my ashes here. This place apart from the rest of the park, as quiet as a vacuum. He's not even sick yet. Won't be for another ten years, but he'll say it when they get home too. Spread my ashes at the canyon. A refrain, just like everything he says is a refrain. Spread my ashes, and I saw the Who in a barn in Frankfurt, Illinois, and There's Hitchcock, There he is, on one of those endless weekend afternoons watching movies at his house, a trick the girls think is particular to him, just as they think every joke is his original own.

Hitchcock stepping onto a train, Hitchcock winding a clock. Spread my ashes here, he says, and they will years later. They'll let some go at the edge of the canyon and some down at its river and some they will put into a campfire in the Rockies and some the middle sister will put into her mouth —a lick of her finger, a dip, and another lick when her sisters aren't looking. The act will feel performative, purely symbolic, but she won't know what else to do. Wanting her actions to mean something more than what she can give to them. Somewhere inside her grief, she will ask herself what is the worst thing she would have done to reverse his sickness, to have provided some momentary relief. She will have heard stories of what mothers have done to soothe their colicky sons, and in her mind's eye she will see herself bent over him in his hospital bed. She will feel at once alone in her imagined sacrifice but also closer to her father than she will when she's actually with him. The same way she will imagine a scene in which she and her sisters are kidnapped by a group of faceless men—a dark basement, a locked door— and she will say, Me. Whatever you're going to do to them, only me.

In the evening, they go into their separate spaces. The father into the woods. The girls into the cool, echoey bathroom. They walk to and from the site together, flashlights bouncing along the small, curving path. There are more stars there than at home, the sky messy with them, and the girls are in awe. Whispering in the dark, the middle feels a silent fear they won't find their way back, but just moments later they see their father at the picnic table in front of the fire. The girls go to bed and he stays up. Some hours later, the middle sister wakes. On the foldout bed next to the oven, the oldest sister is lost inside a mess of blankets, her face barely perceptible within her dark swirl of hair. Hateful and tender, the middle stands above her and a thought, perfectly formed, sprouts within her: It is easier to love you like this. She pulls back the drapes over the window in the door and pads out in socked feet. The father is smoking a cigarette and in his exhale says, Hey, little lady. She sits across from him on a log, and they stare into the fire, the light reflecting off his glasses so that his eyes cannot be seen. She wants to crawl into his lap or sit beside him, lean into his torso, but she feels shy with him now. Their talk is spare and quiet, minutes or hours passing, until he lets the red fire dim and smoke.

BLACK BOX

AD WANTED TO SHOW US his infinity box. It was
Christmas and my sister, Carla, her husband, and
my man and I were in the suburbs at my cousin's. I had
poured myself one glass of wine after another while my
uncle told me where to buy the cheapest gas. I no longer
drove. By the time Dad mentioned the mysterious box,
I had dipped into a drunkenness that felt shut up and
deeply personal.

Come over to the house, Dad said. It'll take five
minutes.

Nothing with Dad took five minutes. He was susceptible to obsession, frequently infused with urgency for a project that had taken him over. It didn't end until he'd roped in someone else.

In the bathroom Carla and I stood before its brightly lit mirror. She was in an advanced state of pregnancy. Everything looked the same—her sleek blonde hair, rosy cheeks, pert nose—except for her belly. It appeared constructed, like one of those grassy burial mounds downstate. When we'd first arrived, my aunt, a retired accountant who cut her own hair in a blunt schoolmarm, had placed her hands on Carla's stomach, and with eyes closed like a fortune-teller, nodded and said, A new beginning.

We should get back home, I said. You know how he gets.

I'd grown anxious and wanted to dissolve into a more familiar state.

I know, Carla said. I'm pretty tired.

She rubbed her stomach, the very thing she promised she wouldn't do. She'd paid an enterprising doula an outrageous sum for homemade anti-stress pregnancy tea, the tint and odor of rotten eggplant, and had been ostentatiously chugging it throughout dinner. I'd helped her to a glug of Chianti every time I got myself a glass, deepening the tea's dark color. She either didn't notice or pretended not to, but after pie, she sighed and said, I feel so much more *relaxed*.

I'm pretty tired too, I said, stroking my gut.

But we can't not go, she said.

Carla and I lived in the same city a little over an hour away. Later she and her husband, Tom, would watch the latest *Top Chef* and go to bed, while I suggested to Jay that the two of us find a bar full of Christmas rejects to play pool with. Dad would end the night eating chips and dozing in front of a PBS murder mystery. We knew a version of this had become his reality this past year— and to me it sounded like a kind of bliss, an isolation you could really sink your teeth into—and yet. And yet he must have had his own feelings about it.

Oh, Dad, Carla said. Oh, sigh.

You always say, *Oh, sigh*. Why not just sigh?

She squinted at me. Your lips are all purple.

WE COULD HEAR the television as we walked up— Jay, me, Carla, and Tom. A laugh track pulsed through the door. The wind slapped me into an unwelcome awareness.

Hello, hello, Dad said, letting us in. Between his stick-straight hair gone gray and wire glasses forever in need of alignment, he looked like a community college physics instructor. In truth, he had been one of those baby boomers occupied with any manual labor that had kept our stomachs filled and his hands busy. He shuffled into the living room and, digging a remote out of his chair, muted the television. The resulting quiet compressed the room in a fast inhale. Each visit revealed the progression of a silent, certain spreading, as an anesthetic weighting one's limbs. Surfaces grew new objects: cellophane bags of processed foodstuff Mom would not have bought and glossy magazines whose covers bore menacing interrogatives—*Are Russians Reading Your Email Right Now? With Impending Food Crisis, Will Humans Be Forced to Eat Dirt? What Plans Does the Galaxy Have for Earth?*

Dad led us to the wall in the dining room. On it there was a wooden spoon the length of a cane, a cross-stitch of a brown squirrel, and, at head height, a wooden box. Its walnut frame surrounded a square of black glass that reflected back to us colorless versions of ourselves. From the bottom right corner of the box hung a white electrical cord that ran behind the chest where Dad kept his cribbage set and playing cards. He flipped a switch on the cord, and a square of lights lit up around the box's inner perimeter. Inside the lights, what was once dull became a glossy darkness that unfolded in a series of illuminated squares, deeper and deeper, as though an unending hallway.

Cool, Tom said.

You made this? Carla asked.

I did indeed, Dad said.

That's really neat, she said.

Jay leaned in, bending his knees into a standing squat. He had the wide stance of a veteran ballplayer. He worked as an office building's facilities manager and was used to taking things apart and putting them together.

What do we have here? he said. Two-way mirror?

Maybe, Dad said, smiling.

LED lights?

Dad squinted. What's your name again?

At dinner, the two of them had talked about fermentation for half an hour before Dad realized that Jay belonged to me and not my cousin.

Carla said, It's *Jay*, Dad.

Andie tells me you like to make things, said Jay.

I've got a whole workshop. I'll take you down into my basement sometime.

I would *love* to get into your basement.

I stared into the box and blinked. The lights fuzzed then realigned to illuminate the box's depth, the line of them pointing farther and farther away. It was really quite pretty.

Billions and *billions*, Jay intoned.

Sagan? Dad asked. Jay nodded and Dad patted his

shoulder. We had been watching *Cosmos* and were filling our silences with Carl Sagan impressions.

So what's the point of this, Dad? Carla asked.

Well, you know. He eyed Jay. I looked at Carla and back to Dad. The lights twinkled in stars off his glasses.

Just a neat thing to look at.

IT HAD ALL GONE a little something like this: There was golf on the television and a bunch of us sitting around. Me, Dad, Carla, Tom, aunts, cousins. They'd moved the couch into the dining room, a wheeled bed where the couch had been, Mom in the bed. For two weeks, Dad performed a circuit. He stood touching Mom's ankles, went into the kitchen, ate a chip, descended into the basement to work, came back upstairs, ate a chip, went into the living room, touched Mom's ankles. I found myself in the corner by the TV, ceding the spot nearest the bed to someone more aggressively watchful. Her breathing's changing, Carla would say. She's having trouble breathing. A man occasionally sank a putt and a crowd clapped politely.

My phone pinged every time a website I followed posted an update. A jet plane had gone missing. Two hundred souls misplaced. Everyone suspected a plummet into the ocean, but I had other ideas: Mom was going to pass from this life to the next, and the airliner would emerge from nothing. Light would flash, magnetic ions would rearrange themselves, and then blammo— the thing would rip out of a wormhole, a wrinkle in time, what have you. I didn't know how the science worked, but something was hanging in the balance, that was for sure.

Near the end, Mom's schoolmarm sister sang a hymn. She pulled a chair to the foot of the bed and told about going on a walk with Jesus. There had been a time when Mom worshipped, and even I recognized the refrain, but she hadn't stepped inside a sanctuary in years. She had preferred walking very fast, and alone, on Sunday mornings, releasing some sweat, and eating as much breakfast as she could.

As she sang, my aunt looked deep into Mom's face. If anything registered in her eyes it was ironic misery. Who knows if she had any thoughts besides, *This sucks*, the last words she'd spoken to me before falling into her uncomfortable silence. My aunt's voice rose to an ungodly high. I tried to step into an emotion that that kind of thing might have unlocked, but I couldn't do it. She was an awful singer. I shot a look to Carla that said, *If you ever sing when I'm dying it had better be Talking Heads or Nirvana or full-on ironic ABBA and not some schmaltz I don't believe in anymore.* Her face reflected all the pain— high and low—that the situation merited. I appreciated her very much in that moment. The difference between us is that just then she started crying and I stepped outside.

I wandered down the block. I thought, Isn't life funny? A woman's about to slip out of the world, but it really is a beautiful day. It was warm for December— sun and breeze and whatnot. Cars were driving, squirrels were squirreling, everyone was going about their business just the same. It all countered but not quite erased the emotional disturbance I was feeling, like when people hang piney discs from the rearviews of their smoke-ridden cars.

When I returned, everyone's eyes were freshly red.

She's gone, honey, my aunt said. She's gone.

I missed it, I said. Like falling asleep before midnight on New Year's.

We went through the usual arrangements. My aunt sang her hymn in front of a black-clad crowd, and Dad, Carla, and I split a large jar of gray dust. A week later, aquatic experts surveyed a cloudy square of ocean floor, but all they found were a few pieces of silver wing sunk deep to its fathomless bottom.

CARLA CALLED the day after Christmas, her voice full of sighs and intention.

Dad said it reminds him of Mom.

What?

The box. The *infinity* box or whatever. When we talked on the phone just now.

I walked the apartment, from front to back. Jay said he'd take me out for dinner when he got home. I hadn't been gainfully employed for some time, and I'd been spending my days taking baths and listening to men jackhammer who-knows-what across the street. I was ready to catapult out of myself. I walked into the kitchen and moved the dishes in the sink.

You don't think that's weird? she said.

I found a block of cheese in the refrigerator, ripping off chunks and stuffing them into my mouth. I said, He's probably just thinking metaphorically.

Metaphorically? About your *wife*? Why not just put up some pictures?

Why don't you suggest that?

You could. You should call him. He always says that he never hears from you. You know, in his own cheerful, nothing-ever-really-bothers-me sort of way.

I just saw him.

Before that.

I picked up the cheese brick and let it fall on the counter in dull, loud thuds.

Hey, I should run, Carla. Gotta get dinner on the table!

My man wouldn't like the crumbs, but I knew he wouldn't say anything. It was just like me to make little messes. I met Jay a few months after my aunt had put on her show in the old church. I'd been doing fine with a number of fellas whom I didn't know very well but with whom I had agreeable understandings. Every few days one would bring over something to drink, and I'd relate to him the most pleasant version of my day, skating along the slick surface of our conversation, and then we'd go into the room where I usually slept alone. I had, at that point, stopped talking to the people who knew me best. When Mom was in her living room bed, my thoughts had felt very clear. I drank pale tea and spoke with Carla in slow, careful sentences. After she gave me my share of Mom's dust, I felt a persistent head muddling. I didn't want anyone to poke deeper than *What did you do today?* Carla insistently noted my absence in voicemails, emails, text messages, and even a buzz on my apartment's call box. I'd eventually reply in short missives confirming my existence.

Jay had caught me alone in a bloodred bar one night when I'd had more than the recommended dosage. The next morning, my chemicals all mixed up, he started asking the getting-to-know-you questions we'd skipped the night before. One of the questions was *Mom,* and I, as they say, lost it. *It,* in this case, being the ability to keep from weeping on a stranger. Yes, he looked afraid. But then there was hugging and talking and, at his suggestion, the watching of a DVD of my choosing. The following night he asked to see me again, the following night the same until it became hard to entertain other guests and even rude to do so. Too I had quit my job, and money was at a dangerous low. Not long after our falling together, I fit my life into his apartment and, for reasons I can't quite explain, started answering my phone again.

THE DAY AFTER New Year's. Or the day after that. Hot hangover sweat, mouth film, and the requisite stooped walk from bed into the living room. Jay blinked at me from the couch.

Do you want to know what happened? he asked.

I sat down, covered myself in a ragged fleece, and shoved my feet beneath his butt. There was an insistent pang in my side.

You kind of got into a fight.

Those girls?

I remembered a trio of dumb heels and legs like plastic. Short skirts that didn't fit the pool hall venue. I recalled asking one of them if they were a package deal or if you had to pay each by the hour.

You made a few comments.

I put my hand up.

You don't want to know? Jay asked.

I shook my head.

Do you want some coffee?

I shook my head.

Food?

Head.

Water?

Head.

Shelter?

I rested my head on the back of the couch.

He put on *Cosmos*. Sagan told how long a Saturn year was, sweeping along its orange rings on the deck of his ship. His sonorous voice dropped me into a black hole.

I don't think I smoke enough pot to enjoy this, I said.

You don't smoke *any* pot, he said, holding a lighter to his bowl, his bowl to his face. He inhaled, exhaled, and offered it to me. I wrinkled my nose.

It's a different way of feeling good, he said. Jay had become so adept at euphemism that he barely said anything anymore.

I'll just get paranoid and fall asleep, I said.

But you'll have one good idea.

Last time, I had an idea for a show in which people were kidnapped, forced to ride roller coasters for twenty-four hours, and returned home without explanation. Another time it was an art installation that was a dimly lit staircase filled with fog and people crawled up and up and they had no idea when it would end and the staircase was so long that people eventually got too tired or hungry to go on, so they'd give up and walk back down.

Oh, look, Jay said, turning. His apartment was on the second floor of a two-story graystone, and the tall windows behind the couch beveled out in a half polygon.

They put in a new sidewalk where they tore up the old one, he said.

What happened to the old one? I asked.

Dunno.

I started tearing up thinking about it. I went into the bathroom, where I kept a bottle of Listerine filled with off-brand whiskey under the sink. I did my worst in private. I was losing memories before I had them. I took a swig and looked at myself in the mirror. I sat on the toilet and took another pull. The floorboards in the hallway creaked, and Jay's knock came, like I knew it would, then, Hey, Andie. He always said it the same way: concerned with not sounding overly concerned. I used to love watching him come out of the shower. Those few moments when he'd zip himself into jeans and walk the apartment damp and shirtless. It had nothing to do with his body or how it looked, but rather how he lived inside of it. Ragged, like how some men toss logs into the bed of an old truck, not worried if they beat it up. It had given me the feeling of, if not security, then sturdiness. Like it wouldn't be easy to knock him over.

You okay in there?

Yes, I said, running the bathwater.

I heard the door creak as Jay leaned against it and slid down.

I always said I didn't want to have a baby, he said. I was afraid I'd crush it or something. But now I know that I can take care of things. And eventually the child would take care of itself. Take the training wheels off, you know?

Can we talk about this later?

Your sister seems so happy, he said.

I thought that she was more impermeable than happy. She whisked bad news right off of her. Maybe that's what being happy meant.

It might be a good time to think about what we're doing, why we're doing it, he said.

He kept on as the tub filled. I took off my clothes and lay down in the water, submerging my ears so that every sound came to me muffled and from a distance.

I PREFERRED THE OLD WAYS of communicating or not communicating, so the next day after my baths, I wrote Daddy a letter.

Dearest Father,
Hello! How are things? It was nice seeing you at

Christmas—and your box of light and how much you still like eating mashed potatoes. I'm sorry I didn't get you a present. We should certainly get together more often. I miss you. I miss the way you like to tell the same jokes and stories over and over. Your eyes had a way of revealing nearly everything. Or nothing! Do you think it's possible to ever really know a person? I like the way you made me think about that. I like how you thought jokes were more real than the truth. And how you liked going on walks. And how you never wore dresses. Because you didn't want to! I miss you every single day.

Very best to you and yours,
Andie

CARLA PICKED ME UP in her tan SUV. I thought, You were a mom before you were a mom. Her belly was nearing the steering wheel.

He hasn't been answering his phone, she said. Haven't you noticed?

I looked out the window. Snow wisped along the edges of the interstate. Dad hadn't replied to my letter, which I took to mean not a whole lot.

True, she said, you're more of a call *answerer* than a call *maker*.

I shrugged.

And even then, she said, rubbing her stomach.

So is that like your personal genie in a bottle? Are you making a wish every time you do that?

Well, *you're* still here.

When we got to Dad's, Carla knocked, called, then used her key. The air was close and still inside. There was a half-eaten sandwich on a paper towel near Dad's chair, mugs caramelized with coffee residue beside it, and in the dining room, the lights of the infinity box glowing dully, the wooden side warm to the touch. It was vaguely reassuring.

Dad? Carla called out.

Hey, Dad, I said, like I was calling a dog.

We peeked into the bedroom, his closet-sized office, and my old bedroom, which had become Mom's old sewing room, which had become a collection of lopsided stacks of magazines and plastic tubs filled with fabric. The dust smell of the old calico was as memory-inducing as an LSD flashback.

We walked through the kitchen and began downstairs. A drill started up and I tensed.

Dad? Carla yelled.

Girls?

Dad poked his head up the stairs. It looked like he'd just woken from a nap or was in the midst of flaming out on a cocaine binge.

Um, let me come up there.

Dad, what's going on?

I followed Carla down.

He disappeared from view.

Go back upstairs, girls. There's, uh, broken glass down here.

We curved around the bottom of the stairs to find Dad shuffling backward into an eight-foot-tall metal cube with a polygon top; it came to a point that nearly grazed the ceiling. He hung his head and clasped his hands in front of him.

Dad, what is that? Carla asked.

It's nothing. Just a project. He scratched the back of his head. He was wearing an old quilted housecoat, and his glasses were cloudy with dust.

The thing had a bulky crudeness—like a metal playhouse or toy spaceship a child might construct from refrigerator boxes—though, to Dad's credit, the seams were sealed with dark caulk and it was rather shiny, which held a hypnotizing allure. He turned his back to us, hands on hips, then back around. His face wavered between sheepish and defeated.

I'm not quite finished yet.

What *is* it? Carla asked, circling around it and stepping over a pile of laundry to the back.

Oh, no, don't, Dad said.

Andie, c'mere.

Carla stood hunched inside the thing. I ducked in beside her. The interior panels were made of the same dark, oily glass as Dad's box upstairs, the floor and ceiling seams lined with the same dim lights. Balled in a corner were candy wrappers and a deep-blue sleeping bag. I imagined zipping myself up in its dark womb and staying there for as long as my body lasted. One year, Mom and Dad and Carla and I drove downstate for the fair. Elephant ears and lemon shakeups and farm equipment flea markets and the Gravitron. The thing spun and spun before the floor was released and our bodies stuck to the wall. But Dad hadn't stuck. Or he had at first, then he inched down the rubber wall until his feet hit bottom and stood in the unmoving middle while the rest of us whirled around him.

Oh, Dad, said Carla.

He was standing just outside the entrance.

I didn't think you'd understand it.

Sure we do, Dad, she said, stepping out to him, touching his shoulder. Dad, how about you come upstairs with us? Get some daylight. We'll fix you something to eat. She was leading him away by the shoulders, as though the thing were a murder scene.

I don't want to trouble you, he said. I can fix my own food.

I know, but sometimes it's nice when someone else does it for you, she replied.

I watched the two of them trudge upstairs. I felt very tired.

WE STRAIGHTENED UP his magazines, ran a damp rag over the bathroom's surfaces, and threw away anything iffy in the fridge. Carla made him a grilled cheese while I heated a can of soup. He ate it all dutifully at the kitchen table, telling us both what wonderful chefs we were.

In the car, we waved to Dad's shape, visible behind the storm window. Carla drove slowly out of town, switching on her headlights on the highway.

We need to do something.

I'm not so sure, I said.

Andie.

Look, he's happy, he's eating, he's alive.

He's *not* happy.

He's alive.

It's not healthy. Sleeping in that metal box.

Who's to say really?

We need to do something.

I say we leave well enough alone. Maybe he just wants to disappear a little.

Come on, Andie. I need your help here. She put her hand to her stomach, moving it back and forth.

Why are you doing that?

What?

Rubbing your stomach like that.

It feels good. It comforts me.

She kept her gaze ahead of us. The snow fell in fat globs and disintegrated on the car windows. On the bean and corn fields, it was accumulating into something like winter.

You know, you disappeared, she said. I never saw you. You didn't take my calls.

I didn't take *anyone's* calls.

I'm not anyone, she said.

She had a point, but it was dumb fighting in a car. Especially an SUV.

How fast are you going? I said. You're driving like a goddamned grandma.

CARLA DROPPED ME OFF without a word outside Jay's building. I watched her vehicle disappear down the street. Or rather, I watched it until it was too far away to see, which is, I suppose, different from disappearing, but not by much. I preferred the idea of her hurting me more than I had her, but such a thing was nearly impossible to quantify. Before I'd left that afternoon, Jay had taken my hand and, sick with seriousness, said, Let's talk when you get back. I imagined him choosing one of three acts: suggesting we bind ourselves together until one of us disappeared, banishing me into the cold like a Dickens orphan, or performing a one-man intervention. None was preferable. I walked through the park and into the neighborhood center. My subway line was half-elevated, half-underground. I liked when it emerged; I liked when it went under. I had a little bit of money left. I could live for a while and not talk to anyone. Just ride the train like people do. In the grand scheme of things—even in the minor scheme of things—it wasn't a big deal. One speck of a person. I thought of Carl Sagan saying, *Billions and billions.* I thought of Carl Sagan saying, *We are made of star stuff.* I thought of Carl Sagan wearing a turtleneck, the most reassuring and restricting of all the necks. I wondered about the odds of the entire car dissolving from existence like certain infamous airliners in the ocean. I took the train as far north as it would go, getting off in a border neighborhood that people didn't always feel safe in. There were alley robbings and assaults and too many men hanging out on the street with bad purpose.

The light was leaking from the day, bleeding out on the snow. It pained me how fast it went from white to dirty gray. I went inside the first bar I saw: an old one, familiar in its dark normalcy. Red and silver metallic garland in the shape of canes hung from the deep wood ceiling. Christmas lights looped down in half circles behind the bar. I found a spot in the corner, where I could see the few faces down the line. The short, bald man in glasses behind the bar walked the length of it to me.

Hello, there, stranger. Where ya been? he asked.

Oh, I—

You're not cheating on me with another bar, are ya?
He was holding eye contact with me, as he'd done many times before with someone else.

Well, no, I wouldn't do that.

Haven't seen you around.

I've been busy.

Well, welcome back. What can I getcha?

You know what I like.

He nodded, then rapped the bar with his fist and walked down to the other end. A few stools away was a middle-aged man in a blue baseball cap. He was buttoned up in a tan canvas jacket, as though he'd just arrived, but his posture—his head to the top of the bar—said that he'd been there for hours, if not years. So convincing was his look and manner—wrinkles deep, eye drooping wetly—that he could have been a character actor for Rummy or Barfly or Hopeless Regular. Beside him was a taller, straighter-sitting man wearing a newsboy cap, his face handsome in the lithe way of a snake or ferret.

They were talking about rock climbing.

You put your line in the rock, you get it secure, but there's no guarantee it's gonna hold, the tall man said.

The slumped man was nodding into his beer.

I know, I know, he said. He did not look like a rock climber. He looked barely able to climb onto a stool. The tall man looked like any other city folk, his arms made to hang from subway car slings. But they kept using words I didn't know.

The bartender returned, slid my drink before me, and retreated. It had the milky opacity of clay water.

Hey, miss. Hey, miss, the tall man said. He was holding his beer can out. Cheers to you, he said. I'm getting my buzz on.

His dark pupils were already swimming in red. Cheers, he said again. He was too far away and the corner of the bar was between us, so I lifted my glass to my chin, looking at him then the other, before taking a sip. It was as sweet and thick as a child's safety-capped medicine. Someone who looked like me liked this, enough to where she was remembered here. I drank it to figure out what it was.

But anyway, the tall man said. I was on that rock face and it was *straight up*. I was basically hanging on with just my body.

Oh, man, said the other.

You wanna know what else is crazy?

What?

My son is in a coma.

What did *he* get into?

Put his trust in the wrong people's hands.

The other man nodded.

They don't know what's gonna happen and his mom, my ex-wife, is out of her mind with it.

Yeah, the other man nodded.

She's a crazy bitch, and I can't take it.

The other man shook his head.

So listen, man. How is it getting laid in this neighborhood? You know some women around here?

The hunched man raised his eyes to me. I looked away and back. They shoved their heads together, their voices dipping low. They needn't have been so shy. The man wanted to find a woman to pour his grief into, and who could blame him for that?

When the hunched man stood, two hands on the bar to push himself up, and shuffled down to the bathroom, the other man called to the bartender.

Hey, hey. Can I get some shots? He held up his can and shook it. Can I get some shots?

The bartender walked down the line and said, Yes, my sir. Shots? How many shots?

The man said three.

One for me (he put his hand on his chest), one for my man (he pointed down hard to the empty stool), and one for my girl.

Me?

You're with us now, girly, he said. You know too many of my secrets! His laugh was scattered, broken into pieces. Plus, he said, tipping his empty can down his throat, you strike me as a hip chick.

The other man returned and the three of us drank.

The man behind the bar filled my glass with the same sweetness I couldn't recognize, and who was I to disappoint him? Or the tall man or the hunched man? When the next round came, I laughed and tried to say, My man is gonna be *so mad* at me, but the hunched man said, You're too old to be worrying about yer ma. By the time the three of us limped out of the bar, arms thrown over each other's shoulders, it was hard to remember what had come before or what might come after. The sun was pushing itself above the horizon, lighting the new snow that had covered the alley in its gray-blue sheet. We all three together hugged. The tall man was crying, the hunched man's face was scrunched up, and he was saying, Oh, naw, man, don't be like that. I whispered, Oh no. Oh no, oh no. That's no good. We released each other, our faces smeared with time and truth. The tall man and the hunched man started off down the main drag of bus depots and motels by the hour. I turned and walked east. I looked into the sun, the earth's inevitable birthing of a new day, until its light was all that I saw. I knew you weren't supposed to stare right into it, but with such beauty, how could it ever hurt me?

ACKNOWLEDGMENTS

For their friendship, camaraderie, and valuable feedback on these stories, thanks to Caro Beth Clark, Mike Don, Sara Gelston, Amanda Goldblatt, and the "Werkshop": Alex Barnett, Christi Cartwright, Hugo dos Santos, Caitlin Hayes, and Annie Liontas. For their guidance and support, thanks to my teachers and mentors Monica Berlin, Audrey Petty, and Alex Shakar. And for helping to bring this book into the world, special thanks to Emily Bell and Allison Devereux.